The American Tango

Ben Chewey

INDE...
PU...

First paperback edition October 2020

Book cover design by Humbird Media
Edited by Sue Toth

ISBN 978-1-950974-00-9 (paperback)
Library of Congress Control Number: 2020916560

Published by Independent Authors Publications
www.independentauthorspublications.com

Acknowledgement

This novel would not come to be without the support from my parents, my grandparents, and many of my teachers who inspired me to see writing as something I could accomplish. I also want to thank Renaee Smith and the rest of the staff of the Independent Authors Publications for giving me a chance. Thanks for everything.

Contents

1

Blooming Dreams

The air was thick with humidity, but even thicker with excitement for Kevin. After all, he had just gotten his high school diploma in his hands; at last high school was over. For a few moments he wondered if he was in a dream but quickly was reminded how real the moment was when his friend Bart nearly tackled him with an energetic and manly hug.

Bart grasped Kevin so hard, he could barely breathe as Bart boomed out, "We did it man, we graduated! Thank God I made it past those last few finals, I can kiss this hellhole goodbye for good!"

"Graduation just kind of zoomed by man," Kevin said as he grasped for breath. "Glad it was inside though, was already kind of hot and if I had to deal with bugs it would be a real pain too."

Bart suddenly patted Kevin so hard on the back that he winced before Bart boomed out, "Seriously man where's the passion? You're acting like we are just getting out of class, not passing through a major milestone!"

Kevin looked to the right and saw a gorgeous red-haired woman. She had just given a wild yell and had thrown off her cap.

Kevin was about to walk to her to try and commend the graduation speech she gave earlier, but the two made eye contact before her happiness shifted to awkwardness. Suddenly a larger man grasped her from behind and spun her around to kiss her.

Kevin winced at this and gazed for a few moments before the man broke out of his kiss to give Kevin a wide smug grin before steering the target of his kiss out of Kevin's sight.

Kevin was distraught with the outcome of that encounter, and it was so apparent that Bart sighed before he gave Kevin another pat on the back. "Jill being with Barry still burns, huh bud? That punk is being more than a little smug about it, but like I keep telling you, bro, if she chooses to be his girlfriend, then it's *her* loss, not yours."

Kevin had painful memories flash by his head before he threw out a bitter, "Maybe Bart, but being outright rejected after all that, for someone who has a drug record, still stings a hell of a lot. I guess I just was not what she was looking for."

"You gave it a shot, bro, but as much as you wished otherwise, she just digs other kinds of men. Come on, don't let it mess you up now man.

"After all, you're going to meet so many gals at college, Jill's going to be a distant memory! Hell, maybe you can meet someone at the after party and get lucky, Kevin! You know what they say, passions let loose when it's a major party and all."

Kevin looked as his fellow classmates were leaving and saw many of his female classmates departing, wondering how many of them were ones he would see for the last time before he grasped his diploma tightly. "You're right Bart. I thought for a while it was pointless to do anything that might just fall apart but you never know, right? It might be fun, and…"

Before Kevin could go on, suddenly a husky voice cut in with a pompous, "Come on boys, new high school graduates aren't going to be late for their own party, right?"

Kevin cringed before he saw a balding overweight man walk over and cleared his throat. "Hey, Dad. I know you wanted to take us out, but that can wait till later, right?"

Kevin's father's face shifted red in a flash. "What's the matter with you, boy? This is a major milestone and we should celebrate it as a family!"

Kevin had bitterness swell up inside him as he jabbed back with, "My graduation celebration should be how I want it since it's mine, right? Why is it that my celebration has more of *your* friends than mine?"

"I'm still hosting *and* paying for the event, boy, so *I* have the final word on who comes first! After all, you may have become a man, but I'm still the man of the house, the man of this family! It's for those who will agree with me the most to make it the most enjoyable celebration!"

Kevin's mother glanced at her husband and said, "You just want another event for your drinking buddies dear, *always* have to find a reason."

"*Don't* start now, it's a damn celebration, so don't ruin it!"

"Not going to turn down free food, Biff," Bart interjected. "Don't sweat it, Kevin, we don't have much time till the official after party anyway."

"I thought you said *not* to waste the moment, Bart?" Kevin retorted dryly. "Whatever, let's go, the heat is making me hungry."

Kevin's mom then saw him looked conflicted before she walked up to him. "Do you want to invite Jeff as well, Kevin?"

Kevin looked to the right before he retorted with a sour, "We say hello to each other, mom, but it's been years since we hung out, so not worth the effort. Guess we exit high school a lot differently than we started."

Bart snickered before jabbing back with, "Speak for yourself man, I am the same as when I got here, just all the *more* awesome! And I plan to get even *more* awesome in college. Hell, I plan to get even more awesome just on my vacation! Man, it's going to be epic!"

Kevin could not help but chuckle at Bart's enthusiasm before he nodded. "Just be careful when you go with your dad. I heard some weather reports that it might get bad in New Orleans this summer."

"Ah come on dude, the weather folks are only on the ball half the time and the other half they make it up for the ratings! I am telling you it will be fine dude, a perfect way to kick off our old lives before we go on to be kick-ass men!"

"I am looking forward to the summer to have some fun times. Well, mostly fun. That TV internship does not sound like fun if we are just interviewing town people about boring old town stuff."

"Not this again, Kevin." His mother said as her face got stern. "It may not be fun, but it's important to build a resume even before college starts. It's to help you get a job after all when you graduate."

Kevin's father then grumbled out a sour, "You keep saying you want to do TV stuff and then you moan about doing it? What's wrong with you, boy? Besides, you don't have anything going on anyway, might as well be productive."

Bart flashed a half-looped smile as he pointed at the sky. "Don't sweat it bro, it will give you an edge down the road and all that, and we will still have plenty of time to have an epic summer so don't sweat it!"

Kevin looked at the sky before answering with a melancholy, "True man, but to be honest, I can't wait for things to get started with college."

"Oh, my son just graduated, and he wants to move out already?" Kevin's mother retorted somberly as she got teary eyed. "If I am this much of a mess now, I will never be able to keep it together on moving day."

Bart could not help but chuckle before retorting, "I'm looking forward to growing up too, bro, but don't aim your hopes too high. I hope it goes well, but it's not going to be instant paradise or anything."

"Are you just saying that because you're heading to a community college, Bart?" Kevin retorted dryly as he grinned. "Eh, I know what you mean man, I learned by now not to get too hyped for things. Still, just eager to put this chapter of my life behind me and start a new one, I guess."

Kevin's father narrowed his eyes at that remark. "You're *always* moaning, boy, things could be a lot worse so stop talking like you're some luckless sap in the Middle East or something."

Kevin saw his father suddenly belch and noticed a few girls giggle in the distance. He tried to repress his disgust as he looked down. "I know I could be a lot worse off, dad. That doesn't mean I have to be content with my life now. Look, I'm just saying I'm looking forward to defining my life to how I want it to be."

Bart nodded and followed up with an eager, "Know the feeling man. So far, we have been on the tracks laid out for us, now it's time to make our own tracks! Despite what is going on, it's still America, the land of the free, and I am sure as hell going to show everyone what I can do!"

"Got that right, Bart," Kevin said as he nodded with passion. "I am going to prove them all wrong about me and show everyone just what I can do."

Kevin's mother saw her son's passion and smiled warmly. "Oh Kevin, I know you felt unhappy about a lot of things the past few years, but don't get too fixated about trying to change things. Maybe not everyone appreciates your talents, but don't feel like you have something to prove, things just take time."

Kevin saw Jill go off in the distance before he had a surge of painful memories flash by his head. He grasped his diploma so tightly he nearly bent it before he turned to his parents. "Maybe, mom, but I already lost time on a lot of things I would rather have not missed, that's why I have to make my dreams come true. Well, once I become a Hollywood sensation, being a better choice to the ladies should be more possible."

"Life is one crazy ride, Kevin, "Bart threw out as he gave a thumbs up. "Still…you got to make the most of it. Don't overthink things too much though, bud, just focus on one thing at a time and you will get to where you want sooner or later as long as you don't slack off.

"Now come on, we can think things over later. Right now, I am hungry as hell and sick of wearing this outfit, so let's go!"

Kevin responded with an excited nod before he looked at the crowd one more time, seeing people head off before he closed his eyes to go through various memories. *Jill, maybe I can't do it today, but I swear I will prove to you and all the others I am not an undeserving choice. I guess I can't be too unrealistic, I just did not have what they wanted and that's all there is to it.*

Jill, Noel, all the way back to Alison, I was just never what they wanted. Maybe I could not change what I was back then, but that ends after this summer.

No matter what, I am going to escape this life, the way my life is now. The town TV station internship is just the start of the things I have to do to make a name for myself, to prove I am a somebody. Still, might as well enjoy the moment.

Kevin took a deep breath and went with his family and Bart to celebrate closing the chapter on his life before opening another.

2

Elegant Reunion

Twelve years later

A woman stepped out of the train and into the Springfield train station. As she departed the train, she glanced at one of the windows to spot her reflection, saw her long brown hair, purple blouse, her skin tight jeans, her heart-shaped golden necklace, and all the other parts of her outfit were all in order.

She fixed her hair just as the train left and looked down at the suburb, noticing all the buildings that were new to her. The sight caused her to unleash an uneasy sigh. *I see they spruced up the place a bit; it looks like old Springfield is looking a tad more fashionable, even if it still has that bland feel to it.*

Did not really think I would return here like this, but a paycheck is a paycheck. Long as I don't get dragged too long in everyone trying to suck up it should be fine. If only, oh? Ah, here we go.

The woman saw a plump man in his fifties with a woman that may either be the man's wife or staff member walk up. She quickly unleashed a well-rehearsed smile as the man put out a professional, "Alison Winters, welcome back home, young lady."

"Ah, well, Springfield has not been my home in a while, but

thanks all the same, Mayor Martin," Alison replied as she offered a handshake. "Just wish it started off under happier circumstances."

Mayor Martin let out a warm grin in response. "Of course, we all mourn the loss of Cecily. She always tried to support the town, even in the worst of times. Still, don't worry. You know how the saying goes, dear, once you're from Springfield you're always considered a child of our town, no matter how long you've been away.

"Still, as good as it is for you to return, it's even nicer of you to bring a whole fashion show to our humble town. To say it will be good publicity for our town is an understatement.

"After the last few years. . . frankly we need all the help we can get to get back in the game thanks to the. . . well, I don't think anyone on the planet has to be told how the last few years have been."

"Don't praise me too much; it was my boss's idea really, "Alison retorted as she gave a playful wink. "He just saw a few pictures of here and thought it would be a good fall shoot and since I was already coming for Cecily's funeral the pieces came together, so to speak.

"Well, he is the boss so here I am. I came early to see how things are and give feedback to the others before they arrive."

"Yes well, I know you're used to this kind of fashion thing by now, my dear, but I assure you this is a far rarer occasion for us than it might be for people in New York City or something.

"That's why we will spare no expense to make sure you and your friends get the premium old- fashioned Springfield reception. Ask my staff anything, Alison."

Alison resisted the urge to cringe as she flicked back some hair out of her. "Oh yes, even if I was young, I still remember how Springfield's warm welcomes go. Don't make too much of a fuss about it, I have a place to stay and all. The mother of a friend of mine who also knew my mother, Teri, is letting me stay free of charge.

"Cecily was her best friend and all, so it made it easier to help with the funeral. Unless things have changed more than I thought, you can save the formal tour for when the crew arrives tomorrow."

The Mayor's assistant cleared her throat before cutting in with a jaded, "Don't think our town is incapable of evolving, Miss Winters. In the last decade we have worked hard to evolve this town's reputation. We added many quality restaurants to the town. Its reputation is *just* as strong as Blissfield's!"

Alison looked past the train station and saw many large buildings, including a parking lot that seemed more in place in a metropolis instead of a suburb. The sight produced mixed feelings about her thoughts on her old hometown.

She tried to quell nostalgic thoughts by quickly uttering, "Well I am glad the town is doing well and all, but I think they want to focus on the natural part of the town for the fashion shoot, most of it anyway.

"In fact, the thing that got the other's attention was Old Snappy. They loved the shots of the tree I took as a child and wanted to do all kinds of things on it. In fact, if it's okay, I was wondering if I could check Old Snappy now to figure out what I will try and pull off for the fashion shoot."

Martin winced at hearing this before he tugged his collar. "Sorry Alison, but that might not be possible. The tree kind of got broken during the last hurricane, my dear. It was tragic to tear down one of our town's mementos, but it simply was too much a safety risk to let it stay up, for the children and all."

"Oh no!" Alison said in horror as the news dismayed her. "That's horrible! I am so sorry to hear that. Oh no, that kind of ruins a lot of what we had planned."

The Mayor instantly turned many shades paler before his aid cleared her throat. "Not to worry, Alison, we planted a new tree in Old Snappy's honor. It may not be as grand as its parent, but it still gives off dignity.

"I mean, we of course wanted to do more, but with how much the town lost as of late, well, it was all we could do. Still, I assure you that the park will still be an ideal place for a fashion show."

Alison spotted the town park in the distance and tried to repress her dismay. "Well, we will see, it's up to Chandler, but I guess it would be too big a pain to shut down unless it's a total loss."

Martin then mustered all the bluster he could to throw out a reassuring, "We may not be able to control the weather, but we made sure the park and the rest of the town is quite the sight."

"Don't worry; I know you all did your best. Just show me what's changed, okay? The team will want to know in advance all the hot spots and the sooner I inform them about this kind of thing, I can do other things."

Martin looked more relaxed as he pointed to the nearest set of stairs. "Very well, let's get the tour started. Oh yes, one thing, I hope you don't mind if all the local avenues like the local television station cover the fashion shoot. Maybe even give a local interview? Such a thing may be common on some channels, but I assure you this is a big thing for Springfield, and I am sure the townspeople will love being able to see an interview with one of our town's stars."

Alison picked up her bags and head for the stairs and said, "Sure I don't mind, and I doubt the others will care, as long as all that official stuff is taken care of. Just—have your TV guys done any work with fashion shoots?"

The Mayor paused before nodding. "Well, Bright Sagat was, er, *is* in the TV biz for decades, Alison, and has covered a few fashion events in his day. Of course, he also has a crew and all. Ah yes, I think one of his staff is someone you knew from school. Yes, Kevin, right?"

"Wait, Kevin? *Which* Kevin?" Alison said in shock.

Martin paused as he turned to his aide. "Oh well I am *sure* it's not

Kevin Bacon. Let's see, what was his last name? In any case, he has been interning for the local TV channel on and off for ten years now. I suppose the job market has not been kind to him. But enough about depressing things, let's go over every single detail so that this works out best for everyone."

Alison saw the zeal in the mayor's eyes and darted away nervously before she glanced again at some of the restaurants around her with closed signs. She saw it was the only one that seemed to be open. "Oh of course, but maybe we can eat while we cover that? I'd rather not miss anything due to being hungry."

"Of course, Alison, just tell us what you're in the mood for."

Alison let the mayor lead her out of the train station before she glanced at some of the boarded-up restaurants, resulting in her mind recalling when she was last walking on the block. *Well, I suppose they are serious about needing help to get sponsors that will upgrade the town. I heard they did not do well after the collapse but did not think so many stores were still closed.*

Well, I guess this won't be so bad, the town must be really desperate for attention if they are sucking up this hard already. Well, a job is a job but hopefully this won't drag out too long. People better not get the idea that I am moving back here or anything. No matter how much they changed, this town is not a right fit for me anymore. And seriously, were they talking about Kevin? Even if it is him, we last saw each other before we were even teenagers.

I am sure he barely remembers me. Not like I am really the girl he knew anymore anyway. Time moves on, that's why while this might be another worthwhile gig. I don't want to stick around here so long that I somehow go backwards. Oh well, for now let's see what memory lane has to offer to eat before I see if Teri's mom is ready.

Alison saw Mayor Martin pointing to a newly opened Italian restaurant and decided to go with the his choice.

As the building caught her right eye, she caught someone looking at her. As she turned to look at that direction, she just saw a brown-haired man walking down the opposite street. She thought about it and shrugged before resuming her walk.

As she did that, the man she saw backtracked to gaze at Alison. He managed to catch the woman strut into her destination, and the sight was enough to make his heart skip a beat. *It really is her; she is even more pretty she looks in her blog. It's been so long, what do I even say to her after all this time? I have to say something, I mean…*

Before he could think further suddenly a snort got his attention. "Hey Kevin, what you doing standing there? Hurry up and get the camera in."

Kevin swerved around to see a balding man with a large beard and with a tripod over his right shoulder glance at him, before Kevin cleared his throat and pointed to a car behind him. "It's all good, Bright, I got it in already, just came back to make sure everything is okay here."

Bright glanced around and just looked a little less bored. "Ah, nice work. Well, that's about it, so you're free to go. Just edit the interview tomorrow and all that. All right, I am going to meet the mayor for that fashion shoot coming up."

Kevin blinked for a moment before he looked hopefully at his boss. "Um, if it's all right with you Bright, can I join you for lunch? Since its one of our next projects I was hoping I could start getting ideas as well."

Bright grinned at the remark. "Ah, making use of what I taught you, Kevin? Or, just want to get a sneak peek at the fashion show? Well, it's not a private chat with the mayor, so I guess it's okay.

"Just remember the usual norms for this kind of thing, you hear? Also, you're going to have to pay for your own food and make sure to call Sam to let him know you won't be at the studio."

Kevin's eyes lit up with new hope as he eagerly nodded. "Of course, thanks."

Kevin saw Bright put the tripod he was holding away before he looked back at the restaurant. He quickly observed himself in the nearest reflection before he tried to look as presentable as he could be.

He tried to get his hair to look as good as it could and cursed after he saw how his bang looked. *I don't know just how Alison is going to react seeing me again, but I have to try. At the very least, either way it will at least be something to remember after all these years.*

Kevin then steeled himself to take a gamble with the reunion to come.

3

The Waltz of Second Impressions

Before the meal was even served Alison was bored. The appetizers were tasty enough, just tasty enough to make her frustrated at the price keeping her figure cost her at times. Yet the taste was not enough to block out the dullness that talking with the mayor and the others brought forward.

Pretending she was genuinely interested in the majority of the things everyone was saying was putting even more of a strain on her, but this was far from the first time she was able to put up a front to fool men in to thinking she was not bored.

A few glamorous smiles were enough to keep Martin happy, and that seemed to be enough for the rest.

Alison took enough notes to give a plan for her co-workers and was nearly prepared to see if she could make an excuse to leave early when to her dismay, another old man she did not know walked in. Alison forced herself to flash another pretty smile as the grey-haired man walked over. "Hey Martin, how's the homecoming tour faring?"

"Quite grand, Bright, Alison is on board with everything and I am just getting her up to speed with how the town has changed since she was here and figuring out where her model friends would like to shoot. Alison, as you might have guessed by now, this is Bright Sagat, the man in charge of the town's film department."

Bart grinned widely before he went right up to Alison. "Nice, very nice. It's been some time since we had such a fashionable thing to film, so thanks for giving us a chance to pull it together."

Alison shook Bright's hand before responding with a demure, "My pleasure, as I told the others, I figured this was a good time in my life to come back to my former home. A chance to embrace my roots and pave the way to my future all at once and help my former town in the process."

Bright nodded before responding, "Well whatever your reason, doing this will boost the town's image, so scratch my back and I will scratch yours. For one thing, I'm sure it will give a lot of the guys around town some local excitement that they haven't seen in a while. What do you think, Kevin?"

Alison's eyes widened in alarm at hearing the name, and her confusion was quickly corrected as she saw Kevin enter the restaurant.

While it had been over a decade since she last saw her childhood friend, she still remembered Kevin's face and nose. Seeing Kevin dressed in a casual pair of jeans and a blue shirt, Alison noticed he looked tired, nearly like an animal cautiously walking into unknown territory. But she was happy to see that he did not seem too out of shape and while not looking like any movie star, seemed to be taking care of his body.

As shocked as Alison was at the sudden reunion, Kevin was feeling even more overwhelming emotions and could barely keep himself from letting those emotions manifest on his face.

While he saw Alison previously walking into the restaurant, seeing her up close, seeing her curious face, her hair swaying in the sun, her blue eyes beaming with curiosity, and a few other aspects of her body all caused Kevin to feel a surge of memories.

He struggled to repress looking like a deer in the headlights before he let out a respectful nod.

The mayor saw Kevin walking up and looked confused before Bright said, "Hope you don't mind if I brought one of my crew along for the briefing, Martin. Wanted him to know what's up so he can be on top of things here.

"Ah, here is one of my crew, miss. He is Kevin, been a part timer for a while, would pay him if it was not for the state of the economy and all that."

Alison just eyed Kevin carefully before she muttered, "It really is you, Kevin."

Kevin cleared his throat before uttering a composed, "Actually Bright, I kind of know Alison already. It's been a while, but Alison and I were classmates. We were friends till she moved away. Alison, it's really good to see you again. Welcome back to Springfield."

Alison saw Kevin smile and saw those around her looking at her with shock and confusion. She then realized Kevin was starting to look anxious before she remembered Kevin looking like that at times during her childhood, causing her to smile widely before she stood up to cheerfully utter, "Thank you Kevin, long time no see, huh? You're looking good, nice to see a more familiar face."

To Kevin's shock, Alison went up to shake his hand. He was hoping for a hug but quickly completed the exchange. The two sat down and Bright joined them before patting Kevin on the back. "That's right; you did say you had a childhood friend who became a model. Guess you were not just making up stuff after all! Well, that's a nice coincidence.

"Well then Alison, it is a pleasure to meet you, but just when is your boss supposed to be here? I figured it would be best to talk to the people calling all the shots."

Alison tried to repress having any indignation creep into her face as she cleared her throat. "Don't worry, I work closely with the rest of the crew, so we can discuss things here if you wish. I came here early to save the crew some time."

Kevin was inspired by the confidence in Alison's eyes before adding, "Glad to see you're a rising star in many areas at once Alison, very cool."

"Thanks, I have been trying to not be a one-trick pony and all."

Martin saw Alison and Kevin exchange friendly looks before he cut in with, "Well I am sure you are Alison, but for this week all of your tricks about the fashion business will be the most helpful for us. On that note, after all we discussed, you think you have an idea on what your co-workers will want to make a fashion shoot out of?"

Alison flicked her hair back and looked more composed as she turned back to the mayor. "I am not sure precisely what everyone will agree on, but I am sure the park and the train station will work out."

Bright then nudged Kevin with his elbow, saying, "I guess me, Kevin, and the rest of my boys will plan where to put the TV van and all the rest of the gear for the shoots. Just let us know where we need to set up. Well, there are costs for all this, but that's more your department, Martin."

Martin nodded before saying, "True enough, Bright. Now honey, I know this part is not on you, but could you know just what do you think from your experience doing these kinds of things, how much of a bill is this going to be for your good old town? We are more than willing to pay the expected price, just want to get an idea on what shape the budgets will be in after it's done."

Alison's face had stress slowly seep into it as she leaned back. "Oh well, that really depends on...Oh?"

Kevin saw his friend check his phone, letting her eyes dart around for a few seconds and giggled lightly. "Um, sorry about this but the person I was staying with wanted to know if I could come over before she had to go out. So, since we already discussed the important stuff, maybe we can talk about the rest later?"

"Oh sure, I know it's been a long day for you, dear. I am sure we will be able to work everything out. Sure, go ahead and rest up."

"Thank you, I am grateful for that. So, I will contact you all tomorrow morning and we'll take it from there? Great, then I will be on my way, the person I am staying with will be arriving soon."

Kevin realized that his window for having a chance to get to know Alison more was closing fast before he steeled himself. "Um, Alison, I know you're going to be busy with the fashion shoot and all, but since it's been a while maybe we can find some time to catch up before you leave?"

Alison paused as she got up, trying to not look too conflicted about the remark. Seeing Kevin looking more hopeful, Alison wondered just how badly he wanted to be able to catch up with her, but also realized she did not want to come off coldly to the others, so she winked. "I have to see how things shape up, but that sounds good to me, Kevin. It's good to see you again. Glad you're doing well. Have a good night, okay?"

Alison walked by Kevin. While she did not hug him, she squeezed his right arm warmly before smiling and giving handshakes to everyone before departing.

Kevin saw her leave before he smirked, happy that his friend from elementary school seemed at the very least happy to see him again.

Before he could dwell on it further, Bright cleared his throat. "So, you want anything for lunch or not, Kevin? Our superstar may be gone, but we still have to plan as much as we can so it's not a hassle later."

"Sure, thanks. After everything today, I am rather hungry, so thanks for the offer."

Martin chuckled as he saw Alison leave and slouch over. "Well, since we already ordered for lunch, I do hope you order your own tab. Just so you know, I have many other things to get done today."

"Oh of course, thanks Mayor Martin. Well, since I am here,

might as well start with the garlic bread."

As Kevin listened in and ordered his food, he tried to look like he was paying attention as he thought about seeing his childhood friend again. *After so long, she still does remember me. Even if we last saw each other as kids, she for the most part seems like the same person I was friends with. Even if she is busy, the fact that she seems interested is the best luck I had all year.*

Well, as long as she means what she says about being interested, should be nice. I mean, not the first time that…no, this is not some random girl on the internet, even if it's been a while, Alison would not be the type of person to mess with me, hopefully.

Oh well, I have to make sure everything works out so that she will want to spend more time with me. Well, one thing at a time, might as well focus on lunch.

4

The Reflection in the Mirror

Kevin's reappearance caught Alison by surprise, but she was able to focus herself on preparing for her coming job until it was time for her to depart to her temporary home.

She entered and looked around her temporary residence. Just as she was noticing what had changed, she heard a squeal and saw her friend Teri run up to her. She had just a moment to see her ginger-haired friend racing for her before she was caught in a bear-hug.

Teri held Alison up in the air for a few seconds before Alison laughed. "Geez Teri, you're acting like you thought I was dead."

As Teri put Alison down, she winked. "Well I mean you were getting late, so I was getting worried. You know how the news is these days, a shooter or pervert seems to pop up every week! Maybe you went home or something, I don't know, I get tense when things go off the rails okay!?"

"Calm down girl, I'm fine," Alison said playfully. "Sorry for arriving late, the meeting dragged on more than I hoped. You know men with power, they like to brag about it and all."

"But you texted me half an hour ago that you were on the way!"

"Sorry, it's just that the tour I gave to Cammy went longer than I thought. I had to go the extra mile to get her to see why we did not need to change where we were eating tonight."

As Teri raised an eyebrow, a new detached female voice came in from the other side of the door. "Yeah…I admit I was not *really* being sold on the whole…old school digs thing. But after Ali showed me that the inside of the place, it was bearably stylish, I think it's passable."

Teri saw a woman with blown hair tied up in an elegant ponytail clad in a black and green jacket with tight jeans walk in.

As the woman took off her sunglasses to give Teri a penetrating look, Alison smirked. "This is my co-worker, Teri, Cammy Jardine. She's going to be working with me in the shoot. We are friends and all."

Cammy offered her hand to Teri as she nodded. "And it's because we are friends that I agreed to this. Seriously though, Alison, if you wanted to save money, I would have covered your half of the hotel."

As Teri raised an eyebrow Cammy chuckled. "Oh, don't take it the wrong way, I'm grateful for the offer. I just feel that since we will be so busy, it would be unfair to you and your family to stay here."

"Eh, I'll take what I can get," Teri retorted playfully. "I mean, honestly could use some more support for the funeral. Besides you gals can get a far better spa treatment here than in the local hotels."

As Cammy eyed Teri coolly, Alison winked at her co-worker. "I promise her mom's cooking is better than most of the local ones. Besides…it will be nice to not have to worry about tips and all the usual hotel stuff, so I can focus on the job."

Cammy saw Alison's tension and formed a rueful smirk. "If that's what you need to focus, Alison, then very well. I'll see this as me paying you back for helping me when I got carried away in Seattle."

Teri saw Alison wince before she looked at her friend's bags. "You said you were delayed because the planning took a while, right? They're really planning some heavy-duty gig here? Guess that's cool, though my parents might moan about more traffic."

"Oh, it won't be like, New York big, Teri," Alison threw out casually. "But it's not going to be easy. Starlight does not do half-ass gigs. But it's fine, I'm used to it by now. The meeting was just extra details, nothing to freak out about.

"Still, might not be so simple. I—I saw Kevin at the meeting. I did not realize he was still around, or that he would be part of the crew working for the fashion shoot."

Teri laughed in amusement as she nearly fell over. "Oh wow, you saw Kevin, huh? Forgot about the poor guy after a while."

Concern crept into Alison's face as she thought back to how eager Kevin looked. "What do you mean? Is he in trouble?"

"Oh, he's not in danger or anything. It's just, I plain forgot about him."

Cammy raised an eyebrow as she glanced at her co-worker. "Oh, so the lad is more than a casual classmate? Is this maybe an old flame being rekindled? I never heard you mention him, Alison, did this friendship turn sour?"

Alison blushed as she played with her bang a bit. "He's not a boyfriend, Cammy, but he's not just someone in my grade I knew either. We were friends, and we hung out a lot when I was here. Nothing bad happened, I just moved away when my parents divorced.

"By the time all the social media stuff happened, we had been apart so long we were different people. I mean, I only use most of that stuff for work contacts and friends I actively talk to. Keeps it simple, you know? Still, he *has* been okay, right?"

"Beats me, to be honest," Teri responded with a shrug. "I mean, we have some social media contacts but have not seen him since the high school reunion. He seemed okay. Still keeping it together, I guess. I was *kind* of drunk, but he seemed quiet. He was always *quiet,* right? Maybe too quiet, 'cause I don't really remember hearing much from him. Not sure if he even moved out from his parents yet."

Cammy casually sipped some water as she cleared her throat. "Well, sounds like that's not too uncommon in this town, from what I've seen so far."

Teri looked flustered before spitting out a defensive, "Hey, I just broke up with a boyfriend and am just reorganizing, okay? I'll be back in my own place in a few weeks, soon as that landlord gets back to me."

Alison giggled as she patted Teri on the back. "It's okay, setbacks hit us all. I know quite well life…does not always go as planned. I had to grit through a few things to hang on myself. But despite the curve balls thrown my way, still on the plate, thankfully.

"Even if it's not quite where I thought I would be at thirty, at least I'm doing what I wanted and not stuck in retail hell like some of the others. I was tense about coming back to Springfield and seeing home again. Well, my *old* home again.

"Not because the memories were too bad, just that, that was the old me. Figured it would be a nice trip down memory lane before heading back to the next part. Just hope Kevin does not think this will be anything more."

"Well, did you imply this would be anything more to your school chum?" Cammy inquired as she glanced at her phone. Alison shrugged before looking up. "I mean, I only said maybe we could catch up if I had time, it would be rather hard for that to give off the impression that I want to date him."

"Oh Alison…I know you were clear, but desperate men can twist anything into something positive for them with enough delusion fueling them," Cammy replied. "I'm sure he's a good chap, but even good boys can cause a mess if they are not getting the message."

"Take it easy Cammy," Alison retorted. "I'm not in love with him, but I don't want to hurt him for no reason. Long as he does not do anything creepy, I don't want to be hostile to him."

"Aw, you're so sweet dear," Cammy said. "But it might be for the best to just take the blunt approach. The quicker he understands you two are from different worlds the better, because he won't get any wrong ideas."

Alison glanced at herself in the mirror before sighing. "I get what you mean, Cammy, but I don't want to be an ice queen about it. Even if it's been a while, I don't want to hurt someone who was a friend of mine."

"Oh, that's very noble of you, Alison, but it's something you have to learn sooner or later. You're not going to make everyone happy, so you have to put down people, so they don't get the impression they can walk over you. If he really is your friend, he would understand, right?"

"Well, I guess it's all about what he, oh?" Alison was cut off as she heard a sound from her phone. Upon picking it up she saw she got a text. As she saw who it was from, she looked shocked. "Oh, a message from Chandler?"

"Ah, so he's checking how things are, huh?" Cammy responded coolly. "See, this is what I mean girl, get distracted by small stuff and you will miss the big picture."

"Oh, is Chandler your boyfriend, Alison?" Teri asked. In response Alison sighed. "Not, quite Teri. Just a co-worker. Kevin's not the only one I'm worried about having gotten the wrong impression."

"Well to be fair to Chandler, the sexual tension did seem quite abundantly in the air in the last few meetings."

"I'm not denying the dude's hot and that I enjoyed talking with him, but don't assume things, Cammy! He's a co-worker I get along with, maybe on a bit of a deeper level than some of the other co-workers."

"Oh, trust me Alison, he showed more than a bit of interest in you much more quickly than he did with me. Not like it was all that bad, we were professional about it and just realized we wanted different things in a partner.

"Chandler does act fast, Alison, but he's a busy man and it might do well if you try and move to his pace. As the son of our boss, his word can provide quite the boost to your prospects."

"Well, we will see if he can pull off his end of the job right before I depend on him for anything else," Alison threw out ruefully. "Whatever, I did not come here to make big decisions, just to remind myself of who I was, to focus on who I should be. Hopefully Kevin will realize that. But I mean I have not seen him in a decade. He can't be that hung up on me, right?"

As Teri shrugged, Alison shrugged back before going over dinner plans with her friends.

But little did she know that her old friend was much more excited about seeing her than she expected.

***

Kevin had just enough self-control to remain alert for the rest of the meeting, but as soon as Bright let him go, he went home.

He was more excited than he had felt all year, if not years. Yet as he got back home and opened the door to his house, a loud yell that nearly came off as a bark from above shattered his good feeling.

Kevin took a deep breath before he slowly made his way up the stairs, cringing as he realized another part of the railing on the staircase had broken apart. As he got up the stairs, he saw his father and mother arguing in the living room.

Kevin saw a picture of his parents, and it brought a fresh reminder of how much greyer, thinner, and more wrinkled his mother looked, and how much balder and fatter his father was looking.

His father was shirtless at the moment, causing his near walrus sized gut to hang out for maximum gross factor.

Kevin saw his father turn to him, and as the older man's baggy eyes glanced at him, Kevin repressed his feelings as he cleared his throat. "Damn it, dad, can't I even relax for a second?"

"Don't blame me, boy," his father snarled out in a second. "It's your mother's fault for being unreasonable, *again!*"

Kevin saw his mother make a wary sigh as she walked past her husband to get beside her son. "Is it *really* unreasonable for me to expect you to clean up after yourself in the bathroom, Biff?"

"I DID! You're just being picky!" Biff roared out. "Always obsessing over little things that don't matter."

"Maybe not to you, dad," Kevin threw in coolly. "But some of us have higher standards of living than a pig pen! How many times have we…"

"Don't butt in, boy!" Biff roared out as he turned red. "This is a one-on-one talk, so don't take sides when your parents are having a discussion and just mind your own business! It's because you're so damn nosy that you still don't have a *real* job!"

Kevin's mother saw him about to cut loose before she tugged him at his right arm. "Kevin, *please* don't make it worse. Your father's just restless from missing so much work and recovering from the operation. We all just need to…"

Kevin's mother was caught off with a sudden cough and Kevin grasped her. As he made sure she was okay, his tone softened. "You're right mom. Well, we are all stressed after your operation dad, good thing you're going back at the end of the weekend, right?"

"Tsk, more like going back Sunday to make up for lost time. Not going to let Maurice have a chance at thinking I'm disposable."

"Good grief, dad, I want you back at work, too, but don't get paranoid. You have been recovering from an operation, after all."

"If you had a *real* job you would know these days that's not an excuse for long, Kevin! I should have only taken one week off as it is. Does not help your mother keeps joking about retirement even though we are nowhere close to reaching that point!"

"It's *not* a joke and I do plan and no matter what you say I'm already in the process of preparing things for retirement," his mom said. "I think having survived cancer gives me the right to decide when I want to retire, and I had enough of all of it. Once things line up right with insurance my full-time days are over."

Kevin saw how excited his mom looked before responding with an uneasy chuckle. "I know how excited you are to be free of your boss, mom, but remember we talked about waiting to make sure the economy was in a good place? Retiring might not be a good idea if we wind up in another great depression."

"That was *your* idea, Kevin. And while I know it's one of the few things you agree with your father on the past few years, this is my choice and mine alone! If the money gets tight we will just have to live within our new means, but my happiness is more important than a bit more spending money.

"I need the extra time to make this place be clean anyway. Wealth is subjective, but cleanliness is next to godliness. Besides, being home all the time will just give me more time to help you find a job, right Kevin?"

"Sounds…about right mom. Still, you sure we can't think about things a bit more? Just saying, having your parents retire before a guy has a solid job is going to forever be a…"

"Quit moaning and act like a man, Kevin!" Biff yelled. "If you just had the right skills, the skills of a *real* man, you would not be feeling so embarrassed, but yet here we are Kevin! You're lucky we are nice enough to put up with this, but you've got to try harder before your life's over!"

"I know that!" Kevin said with raw passion in his eyes. "I'm waiting to hear back from Mister Goldberg on one lead in the city, Miss Cooper for the internship, and a few others, Dad! If I bug them too much, then it will just push them away."

"Bah, you just need more charisma in your pitch, boy!" Biff said in response. "If you just had some more confidence you would be in your *own* house and married already!"

"If it's that easy, how come I don't ever remember you feeling confident at work for as long as I lived?" Kevin shot back as his eyes flashed with bitterness. "The only thing you ever say about your work is that you're just one mistake away from it all collapsing for decades!"

"It's a damn stressful job, boy! Your kid jobs are nothing since you don't do anything but follow orders. You have to man up and take real jobs to get *real* results, Kevin! It may be hard, but damn it, you're already thirty! I was already on track by the time I was where you are now and you're not even close! You have to push yourself to…"

"To *what,* dad?" Kevin growled out as his composure wavered. "Push myself to try and be good at math or banking in hopes by the time I'm forty I'll be able to be an accountant or programmer that has nothing to stand apart from everyone else wanting those jobs? How many times have we gone over this already, dad?

"It's not the same as when you were growing up, it's sure as hell not so easy to get the ball rolling. At least…not for a lot of people. If you'd been paying attention you would know I reached out to so many people the past few years, and the majority of them were lying about what they said!"

Kevin's dad took a weary sigh as he sat down. "I know Kevin, I know a lot of your pals have been struggling too, and that it's nearly as bad as when my dad was growing up. Still, that just means you can't be picky."

"I know that, dad, and I wish I knew back in college or even high school that only a few job types were worth a damn anymore. But since I don't have a time machine or a potion that will make me a math or programming expert or a star baseball player, might as well play to my strengths, right? Just got to keep looking for the light at the end of the tunnel, and hope I find it before I die."

Kevin's mom sighed before she patted her son on his right shoulder. "Don't get too depressed dear, none of us wants what happened to your poor friend Mac to happen to you.

"Just take it one step at a time. It's not a big step, but you got another call for a substitute job at the high school."

"Ah, thanks, mom. Well, at least unlike the county college, they won't be closing the high school anytime soon. One step at a time won't solve everything, but at least it will keep me busy. Alright, let's just put the lecture on hold, okay, Dad? It's not like it's anything more than the same speech you tell me *every* week."

"I keep saying it because you're not doing anything different, Kevin!"

"I am trying different things, but no matter what no one listens, no one even will give me a chance! You know how stressful it is feeling you're helpless to do more than just watch as your life is slowly fading away? But at least, even if it's not job-related, something positive happened today. It's a miracle, but Alison's back in town."

Kevin's mother blinked a bit before blurting out, "Really? You mean *the* Alison? Oh my, that sounds wonderful Kevin! How is she?"

Kevin thought back at how Alison looked before he smiled warmly. "Well, I did not get too much time to talk to her for now. She just arrived in town for a job.

"She does not seem to be moving back, she just came back for a job. Still, it's nice to be able to catch up. Hopefully we will be able to catch up even more during the filming. If things work out, maybe it will become something more."

Kevin's father saw how eager his son looked before he rolled his eyes. "That's the girl you were crushing on till she left around middle school, right Kevin? Bah, don't get too excited, boy. For all you know she has a boyfriend."

"She's listed as single on Facebook, so that seems like a good sign."

"Bah, that's what you said about that Kelly girl last year, only for that to blow up in your damn face."

Kevin winced as he felt a surge of bitter memories flash across his face over that failed romance before he tried to put out an uneasy grin. "That was a misunderstanding based on false information. I'm not going to rush in like an idiot. I'll just see how things are and if things look good, then try and take it from there."

"Tsk, don't go and get excited. Girls can change over the years, boy, your mother sure as hell is not the same woman she was when I married her!"

"That's only because *you're* not the man I thought I was marrying, dear."

"Don't butt in when I'm having a man-to-man chat! Bah, I like when you show drive, Kevin, but being stupid will just cause trouble for everyone. She may have been nice to ya, but not like she was your girlfriend or anything, Kevin! Assuming things can get you in trouble, like it *already* has!"

Kevin winced once more as he slouched over and looked up with longing out the window. "You don't have to tell me that, dad. Every day I wake up and see what point I am in my life. Reality hits hard, very hard. Just got to take what chance I can get."

"Well maybe if you did not always try and hit outside the ballpark you might have scored a few more runs, hey Kevin? A man needs ambition, but you're always been unrealistic about things, boy."

"Damn it, you're one to talk, dad."

"You can blame me all you want, but all those other dreams are just fantasies in today's economy! Even if this Alison's still single, you're fooling yourself if you think she will want to have a boyfriend who does not have a real job and lives with his parents!"

"Alison's not one of those shallow girls, dad!" Kevin snapped out with defiance. "She *always* cared about deeper things."

"Tsk, they all say that, till their college years get more and more behind them and things get real! Sure, maybe a miracle can happen, Kevin, but if you can't get those girls on those dating sites that you swore are supposed to be perfect matches, then what makes you think a girl who only *used* to know you will suddenly decide she's your soulmate? Just look for a girl that laughs at what you say, everything else just fades away quick enough once a relationship gets real. Right dear?"

Kevin saw his mother glance at his father for a few seconds with a detached look before she cleared her throat. "Of...course Biff. Even if it does work out, she doesn't live here, right? Won't that make it even worse? Kevin, your father just does not want you to be hurt again. It would be best not to get too excited and look forward to things that have a better chance at working out."

Kevin's eyes looked hollow for a moment before he took a glance at the calendar and saw just what was, or was not filled in. He sighed before he responded with a restrained, "What do you mean, mom?"

"I know that's been so routine at this point that it's by the motions for you dear, but it's something right? Besides, Bart might be stopping by next week, right?"

Kevin glanced at his high school graduation picture before he chuckled bitterly. "Well, we will see if he does what he says he is going to do this time, huh? Look guys, I know very well by now life's not some fairy tale where everything works out.

"But not trying to reach out to Alison more before she moved away was one of my top ten regrets of the past decade. Getting a second chance is something I can't just pass on or I really will be a coward. Besides, it's not like she said no, she said she was looking forward to it."

"Well, we will see, dear. But for now, maybe we can focus on dinner? Can you get the oven started?"

"Sure mom."

Kevin went over to turn on the oven, only for the switch to fall off. As his dad cursed, Kevin grasped the now broken item before glancing at his parents. "I thought the repairman fixed the oven?"

"I don't trust that guy's opinion, Kevin!" his dad said. "He was *too* nice! It was a scam!"

"But the oven's broken, I'm *holding* what's broken right in my hand!"

"He was going to rip us off, son! I'll fix it myself!"

"I don't want to wait half a decade for it to be fixed, dad! I'm still waiting for you to fix the floor!"

"Well, then, do it yourself, you ingrate!"

"I *would* if you would just let me, instead of throwing a hissy fit over *every* single thing in the house fitting your vision!"

"I pay the most so this is *my* place, and I'll say how things look!"

"Damn it, dad, it's just putting a new carpet over the floor so my feet and back will feel better, it's not the White House!"

"In these walls *I'm* president of this estate, so it might as well be *my* white house and that's why every speck of my property should be how I see fit!

"Even if no one else in the whole world respects me, I'm in the walls I paid for and you're my son, you would not exist without me! That's why *I'm* the king around here, and I will be obeyed no matter *what* you think!

"I don't know why you're moaning, I'm nice enough to not

charge you rent so the price should be letting me do things my way, boy! If you hate it so damn bad how come you did not move out with anyone, huh?"

"You know I was thinking about it with Lou before he lost his job and had to move back in with his aunt! Bart keeps moving from one state or another to be reliable and it's hard to move in with Guile when he has his own family, right? And I'm not moving in with someone I don't know again, not really fond of coming back to finding your roommate put glass shards on your bed for a 'joke' a second time!"

"Just shows how in the end family can only depend on each other, because only family can put up with family! Well guess you don't have much vision after all, Kevin."

"If you had such a grand vision, then how come the only thing you can think of for years is that you don't want anyone else to do it?"

"Maybe if you were more of a team player, my vision would be clearer, Kevin! The sooner you accept that's how things work, the happier everyone will be!"

"You mean how happy you *will* be! And you wonder why I want to focus on something else, when most days revolve around your 'ideas'."

As Kevin looked at the stove, he saw his reflection in the microwave to the right of him, saw how worn down he looked and winced. As depressing thoughts consumed him, he quickly thought of the good times he did have with his childhood friend.

Alison, I know if we were closer that it wouldn't have taken more than a decade to catch up with you.

Still, I know we had a good time around each other. It's, not like those mirages the past few years, it can't be. Even...even if it's only a faint chance, a chance for something good, really good to happen is too good to pass up over…

As a loud yell cut off his train of thought Kevin glanced to the right before he glowered.

"Dad…turn your TV down already! I should not be hearing it from the other side of the apartment!"

"Lay off your old man, Kevin, I'm old!"

"You made that clear by now, dad! But even so…don't take it out on me and try and make me as deaf as you!"

With a sigh Kevin went over to try and lower the volume on his dad's TV so he could think more clearly about how to deal with things in a way to steer his life in a more constructive direction.

5

Where One Stands

Kevin prepared as best as he could for meeting his childhood friend again. But despite his mental preparations and going over things with Bright the morning after, when Kevin arrived at the hotel, he was still in awe at seeing over a dozen incredibly attractive women hanging around the hotel lobby.

Kevin saw a woman in a dress that was designed to look like a slightly more stylish version of the dresses women used to wear when the town was founded.

The red-haired woman wearing the retro outfit caught Kevin's eye before he saw Cammy walk by in a green leather outfit.

Cammy saw Kevin looking at her outfit before she cleared her throat. "Are you lost? Show's not for a bit, lad, so best if you move it along, no time for side shows."

Kevin winced at the blond woman's frosty glare before he cleared his throat. "Oh, sorry for the misunderstanding miss, but I am part of the show. Or at least part of the production. I'm part of the film crew for today. Did not mean to be a bother, but do you know Alison Winters?"

"And what if I did?" Cammy retorted sharply. Kevin nearly winced before he steeled his resolve. "Oh, it's just, she and I are friends so…"

"Oh, *spare* me the pathetic lies," Cammy said coldly. "Like I'm going to throw my friend under the bus for any creep's lie."

"Hey, wait, you misunderstand, I really *am* her friend! I can prove it."

"Pasting pictures together does not count, you hack," the blond woman threw out harshly. "You can't just pretend hard enough and your fantasy comes true so…"

"Hold it Cammy, he's not lying."

A new female voice cut in. As Kevin looked around, he was relieved to see it was Alison. She was rocking a stylish red and black sweater topped with jeans as she stopped to give Kevin a smile. "Cammy, *this* is the Kevin I was talking about earlier, remember?"

Cammy model blinked before she gazed at Kevin for a few seconds. "Oh, this is your childhood chum? Ah yes…I can see it now. Yes, I can see it in the eyes. Sorry about that, had more than a few punks who thought they could swindle their way into where they don't deserve to be. Still…even if it's a small town, are you really the most qualified member to deal with a fashion show?"

"Well we did, er, do have a former fashion model, but she's on vacation. Don't worry, I know enough about this kind of stuff to make sure it all goes smoothly."

"We will see. Well, a pleasure, I'm sure, but I don't have time for this right now."

With that Cammy marched off to the right before Kevin could say anything. Alison saw him looking embarrassed before she giggled. "Don't worry about Cammy, Kevin, she is always laser focused on her job."

Kevin saw Alison was giving him a kind look before he smirked back. "It's cool, seen plenty of professionals the past few years, I'm sure it will make for an epic production."

"Oh, you really have become quite the professional, huh?"

Kevin saw Alison look sincerely impressed before his smile widened. "Well I would not call myself an ace yet, but I feel like I learned enough to make news stories on the level of CNN…"

Before he could finish, he felt a strong force slap him in the back to cut him off. A startled Alison saw that the force came from a large older black man wearing the same cap he had.

She quickly saw he had the same uniform as Kevin before the man chuckled. "Man, Kevin, I thought we went over that *last* month? You're not paying attention when Bright and I made it clear we don't want things like the cable channels and want short stories that can be watched quickly on the phones. I'm the old man, why are you the one behind in the times?"

Kevin winced as he chuckled tensely. "Oh, you know, Sam, just trying to be professional and all."

"Maybe, kid, but being professional for the wrong thing is not really being professional. And if you're really down on being a pro then get to setting up the lighting!"

"Er, right Sam. Sorry Alison, guess I better get to work. Maybe we can catch up more on the lunch break?"

Alison saw how eager Kevin looked before she shrugged. "I—I don't know yet. We have recaps and stuff during lunch. To be honest we get short lunches because they don't want to risk us eating much and all. Plus, sometimes we get calls from our agents or others for other solo gigs, you know?"

Kevin winced before he quickly nodded. "Oh of course, got to get the work in, right? Sorry, I didn't mean to get in your way."

Alison saw Kevin looking hurt, remembered what Cammy told her, then saw Kevin looking warily at Sam before she smirked. "Don't worry, it's not like that. I'll see what I can do, okay?"

"Of course. Thanks Alison, good luck. Also, if Bright or Sam ask any personal questions just answer something related to the military or football, they always like that."

"Thanks."

Alison waved before heading off. Kevin took in a few moments to enjoy how good Alison looked walking off, before he saw Cammy and some of the others walking in his direction and quickly went for the tripod.

As he thought about Alison's response he smirked. *She said maybe, that's positive right? Damn it, if I doubt myself now it will never work out, just got to have faith, and make sure I keep on Bright and Sam's good sides, so I can get a break long enough to have lunch with her if that option becomes possible.*

Kevin ran over and finished getting things up before the production at last started. While it was only a preview reel for future productions, Kevin quickly saw Alison's company was committed to making every second on camera an attention grabber.

He was impressed seeing Cammy and the other models pose in outfits that were stylish examples of the fashion across the town's history, but even if it was because he knew her already, Kevin could not help but be amazed as Alison walked up to the camera.

While she had the same outfit on as when he last saw her, she had added a magenta scarf and sunglasses and as she passed Kevin's camera, he saw her wink briefly in his direction. He wondered if that was to her or to the camera but saw Bright glance at her before he tensed up and focused on going through with the plan.

A few more girls followed Alison before the demonstration was complete. When it was, Bright went up to her and smirked. "Greetings from TV64 everyone! Bright Sagat here, *more* than happy to interview a local that's not been very local around these parts for some time now, Alison Winters!

"Been close to two decades since you been living here, so it's nice of you to have come back with a big-time fashion shoot to liven up the town for a bit!"

Alison waved at the camera before she responded with a chipper, "Oh, you know…I was away for a while, so I figured I'd bring back a gift of sorts. I mean, it's nothing too out of the ordinary for our business. Starlight has visited many towns related to my fellow models, to use their talents to bring out the style in a town so that both the locals and everyone else can get something enjoyable out of it. I'd like to think we are off to a good start, yes?"

"No complaints here, Alison. Well, thanks for the preview you girls gave us, we will be sure to cover the full event from every side."

Kevin saw Alison thank his boss, and nearly forgot to zoom out to show the banner. After turning off the camera, Kevin glanced at his boss, who just looked right past him to look at Sam. "How'd it go, Willacker? "

"A few shots that could use some mighty fine trimming, but nothing to throw a fit over, Bright," he answered.

Bright looked Sam in the eye and shrugged. "Well, looks like it will take a bit more editing to cut everything together, but you gals don't have to worry about it. Thanks again for the show, Alison."

"Oh, don't need to thank me. I'm just the spokeswoman here," Alison said ruefully. "But don't thank me yet when this is just the opening act."

"Of course. Mind telling us what you got planned for the next part? It's just some kinds of presentations require a different lighting, you know?"

"Yes, of course, but to be honest, I don't have the answer to that as Adrienne, our photographer, is still going over what part of town is inspiring her the most for the next phase. But we have the contact information, so we will let you know quickly."

"Of course, Alison. Business has to be done carefully if it's to get done right. In the meanwhile, we will just reinforce what we got here. Hey Kevin! Stop standing around and get shots on their logos!"

Kevin snapped to attention before he nodded. "Of course, Bright, will be right on it."

"You should *already* be on it, kid! You're sluggish today, the hell's wrong with ya!?"

"Sorry, just been getting used to the new camera."

"That's what practice was for, kid!"

"Of course, but that was a test, and this is a real thing."

"Well ya know what they say, Kevin, only when you're in the real thing does a man show his true colors! So, get to it, so we don't have to cut into lunch!"

Sam saw Kevin looking wary before he looked at the time on his phone and shrugged. "Yo, Bright, it's already lunch time. Not like we are in a hurry, so how about we chow down before taking care of the small stuff?"

Bright glanced at the clock and was about to respond when his own stomach growled. He winced before clearing his throat. "Fine, better make sure we are at our best. Go on and get some grub, Kevin, but don't get too far. Still got to plan things out for the next week, especially if you're not going to be around Thursday!"

"Got it Bright. Sorry, just got to get that sub job in to get enough pay, you know?"

"I know you need the cash Kevin, but you can't half ass things forever. You got to stick to a road and commit."

"T…thanks Bright."

Bright went over to talk to those who owned the building. Kevin finished putting the camera away and saw Alison was about to leave the room before he quickly dashed over. "Hey Alison, great work today!"

Alison saw the enthusiasm in Kevin's eyes before shrugging. "Thanks Kev…but honestly that's just the opening act that we routinely do for most of these gigs."

"Ah, true it must not be very new to you, but it's been really new and exciting for me. Just glad I could be part of something you're doing."

"Thanks. I guess it's a good thing you have not looked at *everything* I've done, huh? Well glad you liked how it is so far and hope you like how things go from here."

"Oh, I don't see how I would not like how things go from here. So, I was just wondering, since we have a break, want to get lunch together?"

While Kevin had his hopes up, those hopes were quickly dashed as Alison just looked at him for a few seconds. Those few seconds seemed to last for an eternity before she looked at her phone. "Oh, sorry, Kevin, but I'm not sure that can work out. Me and the other gals have a bit of a review process going on and all."

"Oh right, of course. But um…when you get out later, if you have the time would you like to meet up for like, well, maybe not dinner but like, linner or something?"

"I can't, I kind of have a funeral to go to. You remember Elly? Her mother Cecily's funeral is later on."

"Oh God, that's right. I'd be lying if I said I knew her well after school ended but still, it always sucks losing family."

"Yeah, does seem like that's how it supposed to work right? Thanks for understanding. The funeral was the original reason I decided to come back."

"I understand. Well, glad you have some happy memories for your return huh? Still, hope Elly's okay."

"Thanks."

Sam saw the two talking before the larger man walked up. "Hey Kevin, I thought you were going to get lunch and not bother people? Don't be causing trouble now."

"Hey Sam. Don't worry it's not like that. Me and Alison are friends."

"Yeah and *I'm* friends with Halle Berry!"

"I mean she used to live here but she moved away."

"And I saw Halle Berry at a show, but if I went up to her and talked to her like I was her friend, that would open a whole can of trouble."

Alison saw Kevin looking anxious before she sighed. "Kevin's not making things up sir, we *are* friends. I moved away from here, remember? Kevin did not know my plans but that's fine, just filling him in now. Don't worry, I know Kevin well enough to know he's not one of the ones to worry about."

Sam saw Alison looked sincere before he chuckled. "Don't need to worry about trouble at all while you're here miss, Bright's son is the chief of police around here. Unless it's like, surprise invasion from North Korea or something, you don't have to worry about trouble during your time back home."

Alison saw Bright talking to people in the distance before she sighed. "Glad I know I at least am free of *one* kind of worry while here. Thanks. Well, better get going. Sorry it can't work out Kevin, but I'll get back to you when I know what a good time is."

Kevin saw Alison looked sincere before he smirked back. "Of course, Alison, whatever works for you is fine."

"Thanks, I promise I'll let you know when things clear up. Good luck on the editing."

Alison gave a wave before running off with Cammy and the others. As she did and Kevin waved back, Sam looked at Kevin before he rolled his eyes. "Even if you are friends, Kevin, don't forget you have a job to do. Hell, do it right and maybe you will start getting paid."

"Wait, did Bright say he was going to start paying me?"

"Hey, I did not say that! Don't tell him I said that. I'm just saying he sure as hell won't start paying you if you start getting sloppy, got it?"

"Right…got it clear, Sam. Don't worry, I'll get a meatball sub, then get to work."

Kevin saw one of his bosses give an approving nod before he packed up the camera and prepared to head off. He gave one more fruitful glance at where Alison went, and only saw Cammy and a few others heading off before he sighed.

Well, she said she would get back to me so that's good, right? Then again Samantha said the same thing and that was the last thing I ever heard from her.

But Alison's not just a receptionist that is only pretending to be friendly for the job, or a fake profile created by a troll on a dating site, she's a friend.

Even if it's been a while, as long as Alison has not completely changed from the person, I knew she would not just lie to me, right? Damn it, if I psych myself out it will not get anywhere. Just got to focus on what I can.

Kevin took a deep breath and checked his phone as he tried to repress his hopes and fears about Alison, but little did he realize he was not the only one feeling fear.

***

Alison was not lying about having a meeting and spent two more hours going over all the flaws the women had with their presentation and how to improve for the next phase. After that, she went out to lunch with Cammy and Teri.

After the three ordered their food, Alison talked about Kevin, asking if she could meet him for lunch, which caused Teri to look amused and Cammy to look mortified.

Cammy leaned forward and narrowed her eyes. "I told you throwing the fool a bone would be a problem, Ali."

"I don't know about that, Cammy. I mean, he just wanted to

meet up, not a date or anything. I mean, we were friends, so that's not something completely unreasonable."

"You *were* friends, but it's no longer schooldays. The fool is long overdue for a reality check on where things stand."

Alison cleared her throat before retorting with an assertive, "We have both changed, Cammy, but we were friends in high school. That was not a mirage. He has not done anything wrong to me."

"Maybe so, but you have to be careful about who you're associated with now dear. I mean, have you even looked at what your childhood chum's life has amounted to?"

"Well, I think I would have heard if he got arrested or something like that."

"It's even worse than having a criminal record Alison; the bloke has *no* record at all."

Alison saw Cammy showing a phone that had Kevin's Facebook profile on it. The models saw Cammy scroll down his profile and showed a few random remarks and pictures but no real relationship pictures.

After looking for a few moments, she raised an eyebrow. "Don't you think you're being just a tad judgmental, Cammy? I mean, we most of all know our entire lives are on social media. I mean, he seems like he's been to a few places like France and Japan, so even if those were just summer week trips, it's not like he's spent a decade just in this town or anything. He's done more than I thought and been with more than I figured, to be honest."

"Oh come on, Alison, it's one thing to salvage enough money for a fun summer trip or two, but it's another to commit to more than a two-week vacation and spend a year in another nation to truly get out of one's comfort zone and expand one's horizons. You can tell every woman he's with is just on a trip, *nothing* stuck."

Teri sighed as she looked at the phone. "I do remember at the high school reunion Kevin briefly was asked if he had a girlfriend and said no when we were having a dating record contest. He only mentioned briefly that a lot of the girls he liked were already in relationships.

"Oh, that's right, remember Cathy? After you left Kevin tried to ask her out, but she had a boyfriend already. Granted Brad was a *really* big tool who ended up going to jail for dealing with drugs in a big shoot-out. Still, no matter how nice a letter he wrote to try and win her over after seeing it in a soap opera it was still not his place.

"Though, Kevin still got lucky, Brad was about to send a really painful response to that letter, till he got busted by the cops. Thankfully Brad talked big but not really big enough for anyone to 'avenge' him.

"Still, Cathy blew up on Kevin so bad that I don't think he talked to any girls for the rest of the senior year. I mean it was only a month but still. Not like I talked to him in college, so I have no idea if he was telling the truth about how things went with the other girls he tried to hitch up with."

"Ugh, it's plain as day the bloke is another entitled man who let the media give him ideas of how things worked out. He thought he could just win over a girl with a good old Hollywood speech or something but then realized life did not work out that way only when reality smacked him on the face! Maybe he's not the worst but he's just another fool who does not understand that not every man gets the girl he wants.

"He will just have to accept his place and settle for someone more fitting of his stature. And he will learn his place when you put your foot down on him to end the façade, Alison."

Alison saw how harsh Cammy looked before she cleared her throat. "Cammy, I know you're quite the expert on men and all, but I would appreciate it if you don't jump to conclusions. My friendship with Kevin was not a mirage, and even if it's been a while, I don't want to suddenly act like it was. I, I don't want to be like, like a…"

"What, like an ice queen dear?" Cammy retorted. "Pardon if I'm being too mean, but it's just less pain now than more pain later on. After all, would you really want to date Kevin or Chandler?"

Alison sighed as she leaned back to glance at the ceiling. "Won't deny Chandler is clearly the more fun and wealthy choice. I just, don't want to hurt Kevin any more than I have to. I don't want to leave this town with everyone having the impression I've become that cold."

"Oh, I see," Cammy throughout ruefully. "Don't want to get a bad rep, huh girl? Understandable, even for a small town like this it's an unneeded hurdle to amass negative attention. I know, if you don't want to be the 'villain' in this situation, then how about just let the poor fool undo himself with his own actions?"

"Huh? What are you getting at?"

"Simple really. Instead of just shutting things down and risking him throwing a hissy fit somewhere on the web or anything and have to waste time dealing with rumors, put the ball in his court."

"Wait, you're saying I should set up Kevin?"

"Not set up really, just prop him up and let him show how he is with no excuses. What was that old movie about a rich guy giving some loser hooker a makeover and she showed her true nature in the end? Pretty Gal?"

Teri raised an eyebrow as she leaned closer. "Wait I thought it was Pretty W…"

"The name's a moot point, dear," Cammy cut in shrewdly. "The point was it was about a movie where a rich man remade a poor woman, but now things have changed and it's time for woman to show they have the power."

"Cammy…let's not get overboard here," Alison responded carefully.

"I mean, if Kevin needs help, I don't mind giving him a few pointers long as he does not misunderstand and, oh?"

Alison saw a new update and saw Chandler had updated his own profile, and saw he had his arm around a pretty girl with black skin in a green dress.

As Teri leaned over, she raised an eyebrow. "That's the guy you been hitting it off with, Ali? Is this an old pic?"

"No, it's very recent. So, he's on another job, is he?"

Cammy glanced at the picture before she shrugged. "Well to be fair, he *does* have to deal with clients, Alison. And a hug's nothing too scandalous."

"Maybe, but he did not have to look that happy about it. He looks like he does not have a girlfriend till now, and maybe that's true after all."

Ugh, I'm just tired of the games at times. I know Chandler has his own stuff, but we've been 'unofficial' for over a year. I figured things would feel clearer by now."

"It's just the game love, got to keep up with the pace unless you want to be left behind."

"Maybe Cammy…but at the very least I can change partners if it's a better fit. Kevin…if nothing else I know he won't find catching up with me a 'common' thing. Well, I want—want to know what he's really like these days, and if he's just another guy who's all talk."

6

~·ᴇᴣᴏᴉᴄᴩᴇ·~

The Will to Change

After a stressful night, Kevin just managed to get himself to sleep, and went over all the advice he could gather before at last going to a one-on-one catch up with Alison.

Alison ended up deciding to meet Kevin at the coffee shop she used to go to that was currently called Sweet Track.

Kevin walked into the store, dressed in jeans and the most stylish white sweater he had. He looked around and for a few moments was worried Alison had backed out.

But just as he was worried that Alison bailed on her, he noticed in the corner that she was already there, glancing at some of the pictures in the room.

Kevin saw Alison was in a green sweater with her hair tied up in a ponytail and was looking at a picture of the musician Bruce Springsteen.

As she was about to look at another picture, Kevin cleared his throat as he braced himself. "Hey Alison, glad you're liking the store's new look!"

Alison paused for a moment as she saw Kevin before she winked back. "I admit when I first got here, I was not sure I was at the right place and almost had to double check online. But saw the salon was still the same, so glad my mind wasn't messing with me."

"Nah, don't worry; you haven't been gone *that* long Alison. Max's Mocha became the Sweet Track after Max decided running a chain business was too much of a hassle, and the economic downturn made him desperate for cash. The style's not the same, but the food's still good."

"I see. Well, I know *all* about makeovers, I guess."

"Ha, I bet. But seems like you pull it off better. Well, to me at least."

"Thanks. Guess you're not too fond of them though, huh Kevin? I mean, it's not the *same* outfit but aside from a bit more hair on your face, you look just the same as you did when I left."

Kevin winced at the remark as he quickly glanced at his hair in a reflection and hoped Alison did not notice it was a little thinner than he would have liked.

Alison saw Kevin looked embarrassed before she smiled. "Don't worry Kevin, not everything, *or* everyone needs a makeover."

Kevin saw she looked sincere before he smiled back. "Thanks, Alison. Glad that's not your stance on everything, even if your current job is all about makeovers to make things more stylish and all."

"True enough, Kevin. But some things should not change, because they don't need to change. Besides, change on the outside is not as important as change in the inside. And on that note, seems like you've been through some changes yourself? I saw when I friended you that you managed to visit quite a few landmarks across Europe, huh? I admit, I never thought you would be the type to go on a world tour."

Keven beamed with pride as he realized Alison saw his pictures but then chuckled anxiously as he realized she might have misunderstood how his trips unfolded. "Glad you liked the pictures, Alison. Ah, but to be honest they are not the same trip. I went to Spain last year for two weeks, Italy the year before. Slowly but surely, you know? Was able to get a good deal with a travel agency."

"Oh, so it was more of a tour kind of thing, huh?" Alison said. "Didn't want to risk being on your own? Well, I can understand that's not for everyone, even if it's a more complete, fulfilling, experience."

Kevin saw Alison betrayed slight disappointment in her face before he chuckled anxiously. "I get what you mean. I thought about it, but it would have been a strain on the finances and all. I guess my one friend Bart, a friend I made shortly after you left, has been going from one state to another every few years. He, keeps saying he found a job he likes, only for him to change his mind or for it to not work out."

"Oh, he's restless, is he? I can respect that. Better to take a risk than not risk anything at all right?"

"Well, that's true in one sense. When you leave too quick to have any connections, and have nothing to lose, then it is easier than leaving all you have behind. For me at least, the thing that got me through the tough times so far is having people I know in town, knowing I was not on my own and all that jazz.

"I...I think I'd feel too isolated living in a place where no one knew me, and I had no one I could trust. I know that some don't mind that kind of thing, that's just me, I guess. Besides, vacations are one thing, but too much time away and Bright might think someone else is better suited for his right-hand man. Well, left hand man, whatever."

"That so? You're giving everything to get the ball rolling on what you got already? I see you've been working harder than I thought."

"Thanks, with any luck it will pay off soon."

"I hope so. I mean, you been working for him how many years again, Kevin? I mean, TV is not my forte, but when I see some of the television channels interview me over the year, some of the people

I've seen got promoted in a bit of a shorter time frame."

"Yah…I know. It's…it's just that Bright said that he has to scale back because of the times we are in till things look up, you know? It's always something, but that's the business, right?"

"Maybe Kevin, but if it's not taking off there, maybe it would be best to look for a TV job elsewhere or something? I mean, you've been doing this for years, right?"

Kevin took a deep breath before he leaned back. "I know, it must look really bad, but I swear I have looked, Alison, a lot. I even almost had a real job but just as I was about to work for the radio station, all the DJ's in the area got replaced by robots.

Then…the internship at the county college was looking promising the entire school closed down…sucks they thought another mart was more important than a college, huh? And almost getting a full job in a place that closed down did not count to anyone, because again and again they keep saying that 'Internships don't count and that we need *real* experience.' In other words, you need a job before you're qualified to have a job. To say it's a rock and a hard place is an understatement."

"I know what you mean. I spent a few years chasing after jobs to get my start. I—I had to avoid a few scams. Some, I only got out after I was one step in the scam. But thanks to my father's friend, I was able to get a foot in the door at Starlight. Not like I didn't give everything I had to earn the spot, but connections help push you through, right?"

"Sounds like it," Kevin muttered somberly as he leaned back. "Guess I wouldn't know. Neither of my parents had much in the way of connections. Well, I know moaning about it won't do much. Just got to keep pushing to grasp whatever opportunity comes my way and all. I—I know it's a no duh kind of thing, but I'm happy you got what you wanted out of life so far, Alison. It's an honor to know a superstar."

Alison blushed a bit before she looked down at her bag. "Oh, come on Kevin, not like I'm a movie star or anything. I'm nearly thirty, and my 'highlights' are just being on a few magazines and websites. Not that I'm not grateful, but not quite where I imagined I would be either. Hmmm, did not think I would be back here to be honest."

Kevin paused for a moment before responding with a steady, "Well, I know it's not much, but I'm glad you're back, Alison, even if it's only for a little while. I know you're not like, Jennifer Laurence or Natalie Portman famous or something, but compared to many in the town, you're still the local star. I mean, the way people talk about your return and all."

"Oh, just how many people *have* been talking about me, Kevin?" Alison said innocently as she batted her eyes.

"Ha, well I don't talk to everyone, but you got positive feedback on some of the news articles about you and the others coming to town. Sure, it's not front-paged global news, but it's *still* big news for the town, right? It's all about perspective, I guess. I had to think of that a lot the last few years to not get too depressed about things."

Alison saw Kevin looking ashamed before she leaned forward. "Ah, don't feel too down, Kevin, it's not as easy as we thought it was growing up."

"Glad it's not just me who thinks that. Thanks Alison."

"Of course. I mean, it's not like you're giving up, right? My friend Teri's brother is just living off of his parents and has just given up."

"Well, I'll never be content just giving up. I just got to figure out the way out of the maze, you know? I send resumes as frequently as I see places but to be honest, after a while it feels like it's not going anywhere.

Well, that's why I'm trying to add as much to my resume as possible. I want to make sure your show looks as epic as possible,

Alison, so that it can help my resume as well. I mean, unless I suddenly make a breakthrough with the other stuff, I don't know what else I can do at this point."

Alison saw the dread in Kevin's eyes, and thought about what Cammy talked to her about earlier before she took a deep breath. "Kevin…I don't know if I can help you find a job, but I might be able to help give you a shot. Tomorrow we are having a mini event to placate all the big shots and all for this. There might be some people there that would know people that could have the jobs you're looking for."

Kevin's eyes beamed hopefully as he blinked for a moment. "Really? That's—that's awesome! Sounds like the best chance I had to get a solid link since that convention! Wait, was that four years ago already? Damn…time really has flown by."

Kevin prepared a joke till he saw Alison suddenly look serious. She flicked her hair back as she looked at Kevin right in the eye. "Kevin, you should be able to get in if you're related to the project we are doing in town, but still you should know something.

"Since it's all about fashion, if you want to have a real shot at any of these people hiring you, you're going to have to step up your game and all. I mean, to be honest, nothing's too bad with your outfit at the moment, but it's not really something that oh, stands out in the way you want, you know? It might cost a bit, but got to spend money to make money you know?"

Kevin saw Alison did not seem to be giving a judging look before he rubbed his head. "Well, that does make sense. I admit, I sent so many resumes that went nowhere it's been forever since I had to, in fact, go to anything more than an interview.

Still, my dad *did* say he wanted me to get new work clothes so might as well kill two birds with one stone and all. Still, for that I might need your help, Alison."

"Huh, what do you mean?"

"It's just, to put it lightly, I'm not really surrounded by many fashion savvy people. I try to have a grip on things like that, but it does not always work out. I really don't want to waste money on something I think looks good only to find out it was lame. That's why I was wondering if I could get your advice?"

"Wait, what do you mean? You want me to go shopping with you?"

"Oh well, I know you're busy and all. It's just since you have better instincts on this sort of thing. I mean, you always were the one who knew what they wanted when we went to Blissfield. It's just now that the stores have online catalogs, I thought maybe we could go over it together while we eat?"

Alison saw Kevin innocently show a website on his phone before she giggled in amusement. "Oh, *that's* all you wanted, huh? That store is *still* up in Blissfield, the one in between the movie theater and the toy store?"

"More or less. Everything else around it is closed, but some things never go out of style, right?"

"Classics are classics for a reason and all. Well, that sounds fine to me. You don't mind a girl doing the shopping for you?"

Kevin just blinked for a few moments before he shrugged. "I mean, I'm out of my element anyway. If it's something that's going to be a drag, anyway, might as well make the best of it. Besides, I want to give the best impression I can to make you look good and all."

Alison smiled as she realized Kevin was sincere before she leaned forward. "It's just nice to have someone be agreeable on that for once. You're not suddenly going to change your mind once I start picking things out, are you?"

"I mean, long as it's not suddenly about other stuff, then I don't see why there is anything to get upset about it."

"Well, I guess I do have enough time to help out from here."

"Um, if you have enough time does that mean you two are ready to order?"

Alison swerved to see a blond waitress looking at them with restraint. The younger woman smirked sheepishly as she glanced at the menu. "Oh yes of course. Sorry, it's been a while so just wanted to catch up on things. And, I'm getting there, slowly."

Kevin saw Alison wink playfully at him before he nodded at the waitress. "Don't worry, I'm set with my usual. Well, *semi* usual as today's a special occasion."

Alison laughed at Kevin's display of bravado and after the two ordered their meals, she went about helping Kevin pick out clothing she thought would be accepted by her peers that had a reasonable price. Halfway through their meal Kevin had his outfit set and talked with Alison about how she got to where she was.

The two soon diverged to talking about their time in college, how high school went for them both and various other things they had been up to. While Kevin was anxious at first, he felt for the first time in a while that he was able to be at ease as he saw despite the time gap Alison was still the person he remembered and still laughed at the majority of his jokes.

The two got along so well that Alison and he kept talking after they finished eating. Alison was going into how she impressed people in her tour in Spain when suddenly her phone went off, and she saw it was a text from Chandler. As Alison widened her eyes Kevin narrowed his own.

"Is something wrong, Alison?"

"No, nothing's wrong. Just got a text from a co-worker about upcoming work and things that still need to be worked out. Sorry, but I better get going. Still got a lot to do, right?"

Kevin saw Alison looked earnest and pushed himself to not look disappointed as he smiled. "But of course. After all, we got one epic production to roll out, right? Not just this one, but the ones after that as well. Plus, I got some shopping to do."

"Just remember to not go off course, Kevin," Alison threw out playfully as she winked. "Adding one wrong ingredient to the full product can throw everything out of whack, got it?"

"Got it, Alison. I'll make sure everything is down to the letter. Thanks for meeting me despite all you've got going on and, see you soon, right?"

Kevin saw how hopeful Alison looked before she smiled back. "Of course. I'm excited to see how you look after my suggestions. Text me if you need help getting to the party, okay?"

Kevin nodded and hesitated for a moment before she stood up, leaving some money for her part of the bill, and pat Kevin on his right shoulder. "Take care Kevin."

Kevin felt her squeeze warming for a moment before taking off, saying, "You too, Alison." While he tried his best not to lose his cool, even if it was just casual, being touched like that made Kevin feel happy and he revelled in the feeling before he took a deep breath and paid the bill.

After he left the tip and left the store, he looked at the list Alison left on his phone and grasped it eagerly before heading home. *Well, not the best way that could have ended but far from the worst either. Alison may have changed in some ways, but she's still sees me as a friend even if she's a bigshot.*

And, if I can pull this off right maybe there is a chance, I can impress her enough so that she might think of me something more. If I can prove I can be like the people she works with if I just have the chance, then maybe. Damn it…I can't think too far ahead. I have to focus and make sure I get everything on the list. I'll just get it after getting the laundry, the wash should be done by now.

Kevin was so excited that he nearly bumped into a waiter. He took off, not realizing Alison was at the opposite side of the street. She looked around before she sighed and took out her phone.

She quickly put in a number and after a few moments she smiled. "Hey Chandler, sorry for the wait…. just had to deal with work stuff. Oh, don't be that way, I meant the work part of work, silly. Nothing big, just ironing out the minor details for how things will be for the rest of the job.

Shaping things up as best as I can, all that's left is to see how the others handle things. Oh? Well of course things always run well when you're in charge, but I can't be taken seriously if I rely on you to get *everything* done for me. Besides how else will you get that promotion unless, huh? Oh wow, you got it already. That's amazing!"

Alison went on to talk with Chandler, and Kevin's name did not come up the entire time, nor did she think about him after the conversation ended.

But while Alison quickly moved on, Kevin thought about pulling off his plan every second till he got back to the family apartment.

As Kevin arrived and saw the lights were on in his parents' room, he braced himself for another round of shouting as he opened the door. He blinked for a moment as he realized that he did not hear talking and wondered if his dad was asleep already.

Kevin knew his mom walked often and heard the TV was still on, and so walked up to the main hallway. Just as he swerved into the living room a large male voice yelled out, "FREEZE!"

Kevin yelled out in shock and nearly fell over. But as he wondered if he was confronted by a robber, a cop, or both, he suddenly heard the same voice laugh loudly. "Oh man, too easy man. Your head's in the clouds, Kevin, could have been you not seeing a bus ram into you till you were flying!"

Kevin was shocked as he realized the voice was someone he knew, if not for a while. The man was bulkier and had a bit less hair than the last time he saw him but after realizing he knew the brown jacket in front of him, he grinned. "Bart? The hell did you come from?"

"Other side of the damn planet, man. Well, or Kansas but close enough," Bart said before he helped Kevin up. "Well in any case, glad to see you again man. Still, should have given me a heads up so I could have been around when you got here!"

"And spoil a good troll moment? Hell no."

"He's got a point, boy!" Biff said as he marched out of the bathroom with a wide grin. "Boy, the look on your face was priceless, Kevin!"

"Tsk, seeing your son scared is something that's priceless, dad?"

"Oh, ease up, boy, I knew you were not in danger, so I knew it was a laugh! And I could *use* a laugh these days, so Bart was happy to oblige!"

Bart patted Biff on the back as he shrugged. "What can I say, dude? Always love making an entrance!"

"Guess you had time to plan it, huh Bart?" Kevin said wearily. "I mean, I thought you were trying to get that promotion in that outdoor sporting goods place? Or, is this just a vacation before you're back to work?"

"Not back for good but not a vacation either, Kevin. I'm holing up here till things shape up. That sporting goods place had some fun stories but turns out the boss had a stick up his ass, *all* the time. One thing to get grilled for a mistake, but another to have to deal with a guy always looking at who to blame instead of owning up to his mistakes.

So, between that *and* him lying about promotions to get people to do things for him like a chump, I decided I was done being a sucker for that piece of crap con artist. And so, since I don't feel big on my old man grilling me again for things that were not my fault, figured it would be less of a pain to crash in these parts while I wait to hear from that job in Seattle."

Kevin took a few moments to let the explanation sink in before he grinned. "Sorry your boss turned out to be a douche Bart, again. But on the positive side glad you will be around, man. So, you're back with that roommate of yours? Hope that other crazy roommate did not come back."

"Beats me dude, 'cause I didn't ask. Kevin, when I said I was crashing here, I didn't mean I was crashing at their place, I meant I was crashing right here, dude."

Kevin realized Bart's bags were laid out across the couch before his eye twitched. "Oh, wow, guess we won't have to wait to hang out, huh man?"

Bart saw his friend laugh anxiously before he raised an eyebrow. "Where's the enthusiasm man? Almost like you're not happy I'm back!"

"Oh, it's just so sudden and all, Bart. I mean, it would have been nice if you told me, or asked me first before this."

Kevin's father laughed as he chugged some wine down. "Why the hell would he ask *you*, Kevin? *I'm* the man of the house so my vote's the *only* one that matters! Besides, you keep moaning about how you don't have enough people to hang out with, so why the hell would you not like it anyway?"

Kevin saw Bart and his dad both looking at him before he chuckled weakly. "You're right, it's a good thing, just an adjustment and all."

"Glad you're being a man about this, boy," Biff slurred out. "Now I got a drinking partner again and everything! Maybe Bart will be around enough to get you to be a man before it's too late, Kevin."

As Kevin grimaced, his mother walked out of the kitchen and patted her son on the shoulder. "Don't worry Kevin, it will all work after thinking it over. You were wishing you had people around to hang out with, right? Now you have something to do this weekend, right?"

Kevin saw that with Bart's stuff in the living room there was hardly any room. He remembered what he went through today before the happy memories boosted his mood. "Well, would be cool to have someone to be able to go multiplayer with in the games again."

"I'm not going to have as much time as you think, dude. I got a night job to hold me over while I wait to hear from the guys in Seattle. It's fine, after my time as a guard I'm used to being a vampire. Some ways I prefer it, less posers out at night. Sure, we will have time for some classic catching up before that gets underway though."

Kevin looked at his phone again before his grin widened. "Looking forward to it man, but the fact of the matter is tomorrow won't work. I have something planned."

Kevin's mother raised an eyebrow as she looked at her son. "You do? Oh, is Guile back again?"

Kevin looked dejected at the fact that everyone around him looked shocked that he could come up with a new social event before he cleared his throat. "No…he's still on his business trip, mom."

"Oh, I see. Wait, Mack did not get out of Ratched Hills?"

"Nah mom…after what he did, I don't think he's *ever* leaving that place. Mom, I meant Alison, she invited me to an event tomorrow with her co-workers for the shoot!"

As Kevin's parents looked at each other Bart eyed Kevin carefully. "Alison…that's the girl you used to moan about when we first met, right dude? What…don't tell me you got rejected by so many gals that you're starting to make up girls in your head, are you buddy?"

"Of course not, Bart. Alison, the same Alison that I knew before I met you, came back! Like you, she's just here for a little while. But still, even after all of this time she's still more or less the same person, and still my friend."

"Glad she remembered you dude, but trust me, no girl's the same as they were after a decade. Don't mean to be a killjoy but you're *sure* this is legit, dude? Cause, I still remember the hours you would spend on Facebook moaning about how one girl after another did not feel the same way about you over the past well, decade."

Kevin grasped his phone tightly as he forced himself to keep calm. "I know all that Bart, but Alison's a real person for one, and she's a friend, not someone who was just pretending to get a big laugh with her friends. I mean, why else would she give me a list of clothing to fit in for the group?"

Bart shrugged as he turned around. "Well if I was in my troll line of thought, it would be to set you up for a meme or something. Look, I don't know the gal you wish was your old flame, Kevin. I'm just saying, I've seen this kind of stuff on the internet."

Kevin looked insulted at the remark and was about to respond when his dad suddenly seethed out, "God damn it boy, you're gonna get suckered *again*! And you're going to cost *me* money doing it!"

"Damn it, dad, you're the one who said I needed to get more professional clothing! And you said I needed to do more social stuff!"

"Yeah, but I wanted you to dress like a professional man, not a clown for a show! You got your hopes up for something that's *never* going to happen!"

"Damn it, if I think I'll never be able to belong in a place like this then it really will never happen. I have to hold on to the hope that someone cool like her can think of me as something more than a joke."

"She can son, when you're a real man and have a real job!"

Bart saw Kevin start to look at his father with fury before he chuckled. "Eh, give the dreamer a break, Biff. Win or lose, at least he should get props for trying. Kevin, you can't just be afraid of anything that could be a risk, but like that time that girl was just that so called 'college' pal of yours trolling you, you got to keep your eyes open. Just don't let what you want to happen blind you to what's happening, ya hear? Even things that seemed like a solid bet can turn out to be a sham, as I'm sure you're aware of."

Kevin had a flood of painful memories flash by before he forced himself to think positively. "I know you're right, Bart, it's just I still have to have faith that some people can be counted on, right?"

"Yo dude, what am I, chopped liver?"

Kevin winced and quickly thought about all the times he tried to make plans with his friend, only for Bart to flee off to another state before he just chuckled anxiously. "Sorry man, to be more precise I meant it would be nice to be able to have faith in a woman that's not part of the family."

"Ha, I hear ya man, finding a trustworthy dame is not easy these days, since so many of them are so damn entitled and are all too eager to raise hell at a moment's notice. Still, got to live life, am I right? Just saying, even if she is your childhood friend, Kevin, she's someone who's trying to make her way up. And if people want it that badly they don't care who they have to climb over. The truth is, you used to be tight, but it's been so long she has any reason to give a damn about you?"

Kevin winced as he thought of the good times he had with Alison growing up before he gave Bart a look of defiance. "Is it *that* hard to think a girl would care enough about me to not just see me as trash to be thrown away?"

"Then why the hell was the last time you two talked was before she even reached puberty, dude?"

"She, she had a lot going on and just wanted to focus on the future. I—I have to think that even after all this time has passed, even if I'm not quite where I wanted to be at this point in my life, Alison does not see me as a total joke."

Bart saw the despair in Kevin's eyes before he chuckled. "Still got that anxiety dragging your thoughts around, huh dude. Well, go for it, dude, just don't be such a hopeless romantic that you walk right into a trap."

"Got it, Bart. Hey, I know since you're back and its nearby after I get the clothing, you want to go out to eat in one of the places nearby? They have a new grill that's like the one you used to like?"

"Sure, could use some good grub. But you're buying since my job's not started yet."

"But...ok fine, I'll use the card."

Kevin sighed as he got his car keys and prepared to go back out. As he saw his dad and Bart laugh at some joke, he thought about what Bart just said and tried not to let his anxiety consume his thoughts. *Alison, Bart's not wrong, but why would you meet with me if you did not want to see me? I have to prove to her I'm not a joke. I have to prove I can make it to the big leagues if I just have a real shot at being able to prove myself. I have to prove I'm not a nobody who's already peaked from nothing, I have to, I have to!*

7

Making A Place for One's Self Amidst the Tides of The World

With how anxious he was to make sure he pulled things off right, Kevin double checked every item Alison listed to make sure he got the right piece, and since he knew he at times could get forgetful when he was anxious, he had Bart make sure each item was what was asked of him, a request that added an additional price to Bart's lunch.

Despite nearly costing him all the earnings he made in the month, Kevin was happy he was able to prove to Alison he could be on her level.

After getting the complete outfit, despite some bitterness at being left out of the loop, Kevin did enjoy catching up with Bart and hearing of all the wild adventures he went through in his last job.

After trading a few stories, Kevin felt remorseful that aside from his vacation, his stories hardly had changed from the last time he was catching up with Bart, just the different stories he had seen, the girls he had failed to win over, or even get to notice him, and the jobs that did not get back to him.

The determination to change that caused him to go into great detail to Bart on why it was worth it to try and impress Alison, and to his relief he gave a good enough impression to get his cynical friend to concede it was at least something to try and go for.

After a nice dessert, Kevin went back home and prepared as much as he could, and before he knew it, it was time for another do or die situation, or at least that's how it felt in his head.

The next day, Kevin entered the place where the Starlight people were having their get together, one of the hipper restaurants that had a dance floor for parties, the Frosty Penguin. Kevin once went with Bart a few years ago, but this was the first time he was going past the dinner booths.

Kevin saw a person with the Starlight Glimmer uniform before he walked up to him. "Hey there, man. I'm here for the company event?"

The guard eyed Kevin carefully. Though he was not overtly hostile, he did raise an eyebrow. "No offense, buddy, but have not seen you around. Who are you again?"

"Oh right. I'm Kevin, Kevin Summers. I'm from around here, I'm working as a camera man for the shoots being done in town. Er…I was informed that meant I could attend the party here?"

Kevin got anxious as the guard paused, before he chuckled. "Right, the local help was on the list, too. Now that I think about it, you look like the dude who was filming before. Alright sir, go ahead."

Kevin smiled before walking inside. While the lights were dim, he saw many models, men and women alike, dancing in the center. As nice as a sight as it was, it also made Kevin tense up.

Dancing was never his specialty. While he was more than aware of how many women thought dancing was a vital skill to be good at for dates, his reflexes made him frequently one step behind those around him, much to his dismay.

He glanced to the right and saw Cammy dancing before he

quickly realized if he was asked to dance, there was a good chance his attempt to look good in front of Alison and her friends would just make him look foolish.

Kevin then realized he did not see Alison and felt even more anxious as he wondered if she was even there. As he rapidly thought of more and more things to make him anxious, little did he realize Alison was behind him, finishing a drink in her seat.

She saw him looking around like a deer in the headlights before another co-worker of Alison, Tammy, leaned up to her. "Hey when did we hire a new guy to the team, Ali? He's a bit lankier than the others but he looks kind of cute."

Alison realized that now that he was wearing the jeans, jacket, and shirt she recommended he caused her to feel things she did not even think were possible to feel from him before she blushed.

Kevin really did take my advice seriously. Guess he really wanted to leave a good impression. Well, have to admit, if he just looked more confident, he might not make it in Starlight, but he does not look too bad. Guess from what he told me and did not want to tell me his confidence took some hits. Well, not about to do everything and anything to make him feel good, but can't hurt to give him a push in the right direction.

Alison cleared her throat before she looked at Tammy ruefully. "He's not with us, Tammy. He's Kevin, a friend from here. Hey Kevin!"

Alison quickly called out to her friend before her co-worker could ask more questions. Despite the noise in the room, Kevin heard her and turned around. As happy as he was to see her, he knew he had to keep his cool in front of all her co-workers and just gave a casual wave.

"Hey Alison, looking sharp."

"Thanks! Same to you."

"Thanks, sorry I wasn't able to get here earlier but hope you're all enjoying the party."

Tammy laughed as she shoved Alison playfully. "Oh man, you really must not work here if you don't know what's going on. Party's already started, but it's mostly been for the higher-ups. They will be out soon after they have their chats and give a few free drinks but us worker ants are just here for the background when they give victory pictures for the website. But at least they give free drinks when they do."

Alison saw Kevin looked confused before she winked. "Kevin's looking for better jobs, so I told him he could try giving his contact information to people here."

Tammy saw Kevin nod before she giggled. "Is that so? Well, I did hear that Rodizio is getting fired for going out of control in the gig in Texas, so we just might have an opening. You might not fit his specialization buddy, but if you show you can leave a good enough impression you might create a new one."

Kevin paused for a few moments till he realized Tammy was serious, causing him to clear his throat. "It's very nice of you to think that miss, but to be honest my skills are more on the filming side of things."

"Oh, stop trying to be so modest! Rodizio was found by our boss when he was dancing in Mexico. You never know when you can turn your life around, huh? Come on dude, show me your best dance!"

Kevin quickly looked around as he pushed himself to think of the best response. As he glanced around the room he shrugged. "Thanks for being interested but to be honest, I just got here so I'd rather see the stage before just crashing in and all."

Alison giggled lightly, and Tammy just laughed loudly before she leaned back. "Oh, come on, seriously? If you have something to show, don't be afraid to take the spotlight. Unless you're trying to avoid giving us all a good joke to laugh about, huh dear?"

Alison saw Kevin looking more and more anxious before she cleared her throat. "I'm sure Kevin wants to show all the skills he has, but with that long day and his foot injury he told me about, dancing might not be the best way to start off, right?"

Kevin blinked for a second till he realized Alison was giving him cover to back out of dancing before he chuckled. "Right Alison. Yeah, don't mean to kill the vibe, but always best not to do something you can't do at your best, right?"

Tammy eyed Kevin before she shrugged. "Well, guess that was my excuse to wait on the last shoot. Well, I know what makes everything better, drinks! Want a refill, Ali?"

"Not yet," Alison answered casually. "Want to be on top of things in case some of Chandler's influential friends come around and all."

"Aw Alison, not wanting to repeat what happened last year? But it worked out well for you for the most part, right? Whatever, we will see whose game plan wins."

Tammy went to get her drink, and as she left Kevin sat down before giving Alison a grateful nod. "Thanks Alison, without your quick thinking I might have made a rather lame first impression to your co-workers."

"Just like old times huh?" Alison threw out ruefully. "I can't bail you out all the time you know, but I guess it's been a while, so I had a bail-out card stored up over the years, right? I figured back then you were not much of a dancer, though things might have changed over the years."

"Things might have changed, but sadly me being a dancer worth a damn is not one of them," Kevin answered sheepishly. "I mean, I try, but my body just won't react in time, not like you or others."

"Oh, you're thinking too much about it, Kevin, every time you dance it's not about performing like you're in American Idol, it's about having fun and cutting lose! Still, I remember the one party in middle school, Brad did seem like a jackass."

"Ha, ha, yeah. I think, after I spent weeks being laughed at. I don't think I really danced in public since then."

"In public? Wait, you tried dancing on your own?"

Kevin saw Alison was not looking judgmental before he shrugged. "Sometimes when I visited family over the years my older cousin would try and get me to dance with her. I was able to keep up with her after like, twenty minutes of going through the motions, I guess."

"Aw, see, you can dance, you just have to not psych yourself out. You need someone to lead or something?"

"Well, it could help."

Alison paused for a moment as she looked around the room before she sighed. "Well, can't do anything too involved but I could lead you off if you can think of a song that could work."

As Kevin frantically tried to muster an idea that would pass, suddenly the two heard a groan from the right before Cammy walked up with a drink in her hand. The blond woman quickly sat next to Alison and gave Kevin a judging look. "Alison, none of us have to work anymore, it's our time off right? Sounds like this bloke has to prove his worth to everyone. Why else would you be here, huh chap?"

Kevin saw Cammy giving him a harsh look before he chuckled anxiously. "Well, was hoping it would be a fun night, but you're right, miss, business before pleasure and all."

"Well thankfully I'm not making that decision, though at this point it might not have been a good outcome for you, mate. But don't worry, Carlos should be out soon. Oh, speak of the devil, seems he's ahead of schedule."

Kevin saw a tan man with hair to his sides in a stylish blue suit strut into the room with a striking beautiful woman at his side. The man made his presence known by yelling loudly in a playful tone. As most in the room turned to him, he grinned. "Hey ladies, enjoying the party?"

As many playful retorts were sent his way, he responded with a slick, "Glad you're all making do. Worked things out with Dior, things are set for Paris!"

Kevin saw how excited Alison, Tammy, and even Cammy looked before Carlos basked in the positive feedback. "Really doubted I would deliver? To be fair, it's because Chandler pulled through on his end that it's all coming together. Don't worry, he will be here soon enough. So just put up with this place a bit longer and it's going to be good times soon enough."

Kevin tried to not look dismayed at the sight of so many of the people in the room looking happy at the thought of being done with his town, though, to his relief, Alison did not look as happy. Carlos walked right up to Kevin before he smirked. "Good timing, dude, could use a refill for my drink."

Alison saw Kevin blink in confusion before she sighed. "Hey Carlos, remember the friend I had from here that worked on the camera for the shoot? This is Kevin, the waiter's over to the right."

Carlos saw Kevin wave before he snickered. "Sorry amigo, had not had time to feel the place, ya hear? Thanks for helping to make things go smoothly though. Sometimes the local help half-asses' things and makes things a pain, yah know?"

Kevin saw Carols look earnest before he took his hand into a hardy shake. "I know what you mean sir, I know full well how much of a pain it is when a co-worker does not pull their weight. I try and do what I can so that does not happen when I'm on the job."

"Ah hell, Sir? Not even thirty yet, so no need for that. Since we are having a party you can call me Carlos. So, amigo, take it you're here looking for something or another?"

"Right on, Carlos," Kevin said as he shook his hand firmly. "Oh, can't deny I'm currently trying to evolve my current position. I don't know if there are any spots open in Starlight, but if you know any place that could use a cameraman, I would be grateful for that."

Carlos saw Alison behind Kevin looking at him with a pleading look before he chuckled and patted Kevin on the back. "No promises dude, but if your stuff is solid, I'll look around and see who could use a new member of their crew. Here's my card, Kevin. Send me your stuff as soon as you can."

"Got it, and you can get back to me on my email here," Kevin said as he handed out a business card from his pocket. As Carlos took the card, he looked impressed.

"I see you've been preparing, huh? Always good to see an amigo that has his eye on the ball. So, you wanted this for a while, hey, Kevin? Guess that means you want to work in Fendi one day?"

Kevin realized Carlos was testing how much he knew about fashion before he cleared his throat. "Well, I don't want to be too picky or delusional, but to say the least, I would not turn it down if the chance presented itself. I mean, I'd be honored if I got into Prada or any of the big ones or the news stations like CNN and others."

"So desperate that it's first come first serve, dude? I know guys like you can't be picky in how you rise up, amigo, but truth is if a guy seems like a dog starving for scraps it's a turn-off, right? It's not just bad when a guy's looking too desperate for a girl, for a job or anything, right Kevin? Like, you have any reason you want to get into Fendi other than its reputation?"

Kevin paused for a moment before he shrugged. "I mean, I like the style they have more compared to others?"

"Wow, you want to work with them and that's the best reason you can put out, man?"

"Sorry, sometimes I don't express how I feel in the most precise way, which can suck since I'm also trying to be a writer. I swear there is more to it than that."

Before he could go on, Kevin's stomach growled, causing Carlos to laugh. "What's wrong, Kevin, can't think coherently on an empty gut? Hell, I can't either, so let's eat!"

Kevin saw Alison smile in relief before he smiled back and sat down. After food was delivered, Kevin was happy that Carlos talked about other things from politics to movies and was glad that he had something in common with Carlos.

Not wanting to make the chat all about him, and more than willing to see how the others interacted, Kevin watched curiously as the others talked about their business and was more than happy to hear more about Alison's own adventures. After an hour and a half of eating and talking, the dinner reached its end.

Kevin talked a bit about the filming he had done for Bright in the past few years. Just then Carlos got a message from his phone before he grinned. "Seems like you've done the best you could with what you've got Kevin, not bad. Well man, it's been fun but seems like this place is reaching closing time. Since they were kind enough to let us have the place, best not to impose too much?"

Kevin saw Alison and the other ladies looking a mix of disappointed and excited before Cammy yawned. "Fair enough. For the best, don't want any small-minded local throwing a fit if we were to go all out."

Alison saw Kevin looking conflicted before she smiled at him. "Thanks for making it tonight Kevin. Glad you did not feel out of place here."

Kevin struggled to figure out the best way to respond as he nodded. "Thanks for giving me a few pointers to how to fit in better, Alison. I'm glad I could make it. To say the least, this has all been a great change of pace for how things have been the past few months, well, for a while. Just wish it did not have to end so soon."

Alison saw Kevin looking regretful before she winked. "Oh, don't get so sad already Kevin, not like it's all over already, right?"

Kevin had hope surge through him as his eyes widened. "Oh, you mean the night's not over after all? Why, did you want to do something after this, Alison?"

Alison saw how hopeful Kevin was before she blushed and giggled anxiously. "Oh, sorry if I gave the wrong impression. I meant the tour as a whole was not over, not tonight itself. Why, is this the end of your night or just the start? I know this is the time when your day ended when I was still here, but things change, right?"

Kevin nodded and was about to respond when his phone buzzed, and he saw he got a new text. He saw it was from Bart, a request to get some more drinks on the way home because he went through all of the ones at home already.

As Kevin winced, Alison raised an eyebrow, and as he saw this he grimaced. "Oh, sorry about that, my pal Bart, the one I talked to you about last time, wanted me to get some stuff on the way back."

"On the way back? Oh, so you had plans already after this did you? Guess you did not expect this to last very long, Kevin?"

"Er, it's not like that Alison, I swear. It's just, at the moment Bart's living with us till things get going on his new job and all."

"Oh, you're letting your friend live with you, Kevin? That's nice of you."

"Well, it was my dad's call, but did not want to leave a friend out to dry, right? I mean, I wish he cared enough to talk about it with me first, but minor details are not something to dwell about when it's important, right?"

Alison took in what Kevin said, but before she could respond, Cammy cut in with a groan. "So, you live with your parents like a man-child who never grew up and you have a friend in as well? It's true what they say about American men, too many don't want to grow up."

Kevin saw Cammy's clear disgust before he lowered his head. "I know it's not the most um, attractive situation, but sometimes life gives us a less than ideal hand and we just got to deal with it, right?"

"Yeah, some would say that's just what pathetic slackers say to excuse their own weakness," Cammy said coldly.

Alison could tell Kevin was starting to look stressed before she sighed. "Don't be too harsh now, Cammy. It's not always so easy to reshuffle the deck we get when we don't have *our* level of charm, right? Kevin don't feel bad about where you are in life. I've seen plenty of other people our age who are not quite where they thought they would be. To be honest, I don't even have a real home at the moment."

Kevin blinked for a moment as he eyed her carefully. "What, you're homeless, Alison?"

"Well, not really. I still have a room at my dad's place, and a few places I stay long-term where I have frequent jobs. But other than that, why bother? With how much that's digital, aside from a laptop and a few other vital things, everything else is just an expense. I mean, I was cooped up for so long in the same place during the lockdown, I can't seriously see myself wanting to be trapped in a place like that ever again, as long as that kind of thing never happens again."

"Oh, I did not realize that, but that makes sense. Well, if you're happy with how that's going, then that's all that matters right? I am happy you have the life you want, Alison. I guess we got off topic, but what I was about to say before is that Bart just asked me to get some drinks on the way back, whenever I get back. I just mean, we can still do more or hang out more, if you want, of course."

Alison saw Kevin was trying to play it cool, but a hint of longing was in his eyes. She glanced at her own phone before she gave an apologetic smile. "Sorry Kevin, but honestly don't have much of a night left on my end. Maybe go over a few things for work, but still got a lot to do. Despite how easy we make it look; it takes a lot to be stylish."

"Oh right, of course. I would never want to get in the way of your work, Alison. Oh well, guess I'll be seeing you at the next part of the gig anyway, right?"

"Of course. Glad you're not impatient enough to wait another day."

"Oh, I had a lot of years to refine my patience, I suppose. Still, I'll leave you all to your stuff and be on my way. Going to send my stuff to you the moment I get on my computer, Carlos."

"Showing moxy's always a good way to improve your odds, amigo!" Carlos responded. "You better believe that whoever can get the best results the quickest is the guy or gal who gets the bonus, Kevin."

"Well then, I'll just have to show you guys that's something I can do? See you guys soon."

As Kevin high fived Carlos, Alison saw Kevin was trying to mask his disappointment as much as he could before she sighed. "Hey, I'll walk out with you, Kevin. How far did you park?"

"Thanks Alison, I got a spot in the parking lot."

"Great."

Kevin smiled and the two walked out of the restaurant. Kevin saw Carlos talking with Cammy and some of the others before he chuckled. "I have to admit, Alison, I did not know what your boss would be like, but Carlos seems like a rather cool guy."

"Ha, Carlos is not my 'Boss' boss, but I see him more than some of the higher-ups and that's for the best as he's good at getting things done without being smug about it. He is good at doing quite a lot of things, that's why it's a shame he swings for the other team at times."

"Oh, wait does he work for another rival fashion business too?"

Alison burst out laughing, with enough force that she grasped her arms. As Kevin looked at her curiously, she patted him on the shoulder. "Oh, not that *kind* of team. For this instance, I was talking about which team he plays for on the romance side of things."

Kevin saw Alison smirk before he got her meaning and nodded. "Oh, I see. Not how I play the game, so to speak, but if it works for him, more power to him. Well, glad you're all on the same team in some ways. I just mean, my boss Bright and most of the others are really old-fashioned about a lot of things from hobbies to politics. Aside from a few TV shows, we don't have much in common, so things can get a little stiff."

"I get what you mean. Before I joined Starlight, I had a few bosses who I did not see eye to eye with. It was a pain to put on a false self, but I've seen a few people who always have to speak their mind and keep losing their jobs because of it so they don't get far. It's part of growing up, right?"

"In theory at least. Well, hopefully I did not totally drop the ball with Carlos."

"Don't worry Kevin, you did great, seriously. Maybe not as great as a movie star may have done it, but you still did it like a pro. Just don't stress out about it, okay?"

"Sure, Alison thanks. Well, better get going but thanks again for inviting me and have a good night."

"Thanks, you too, Kevin."

Kevin lingered for a moment and just gave Alison a wave before he went into his car. As she saw him leave, she sighed.

Well, have to hand it to Kevin, he is taking what I said seriously. He can try and hide it, but I know what he wants. Seems like he's getting his hopes up, too. Better figure out the best way to let him down in a way that won't make things worse. Well first I'll text C, huh? Oh, damn it, I left my purse at the booth!

Alison quickly rushed back into the bar, and as she entered, she saw Cammy waiting for her, with her purse. "Forgetting something, mate?"

"Sorry about that," Alison replied. "I just wanted to make sure things with Kevin ended on a good note, Cammy, or at least as good as they can be considering the situation. I mean, I'm proud of him for being so professional."

Cammy could not help but giggle as she leaned forward. "Oh Alison, it's like you're proud of a pet, not a person. Well, I guess this whole game was to see if he could be groomed, right?"

Alison looked flustered as she looked down. "You're starting to enjoy this too much, Cammy. Geez, I just want to see Kevin be in a better spot than he is now and am happy he is serious about doing the legwork to pull it off. I mean, you think he might fit in in some of the places you work with, Carlos?"

Carlos saw Alison looking at him before he chuckled and slicked his hair back. "Your friend seemed nice Ali. If he sends me his stuff before I forget, I'll keep my word. Still, I'll just do what I said I'll do, no promises after that. To be honest, he seems like a nice guy and all but being pleasant is not enough if you don't have the skills to back it up. I mean, this amigo's over thirty and *all* he's done is intern at a local station? Guy's got no drive, Chica."

Alison thought about all the things Kevin talked about with her before she looked defensive. "No offense Carlos, but I know Kevin is not content where he is. He wants to be a voice actor, a writer, and a few other things. But he has had trouble getting things to take off.

I guess in the end the job market was so dismal the past few years he could not make the cut. I mean, I myself had trouble finding my place till I found you guys at Starlight. Kevin doesn't just want to do local stuff all his life, someone just needs to give him a chance."

"I don't know Alison," Cammy said. "I did see some of the videos he posted about his work. Its rather mundane work covering mundane events, nothing that has the spark, ya know?"

"If all he gets offered is routine stuff, how is he ever going to be able to prove himself? He told me that his bosses here don't let him do anything non-routine because they don't want their viewers to feel confused or something."

"I'm not heartless Alison, I get what you mean. I don't want to be a jackass, but the simple fact is that most people don't have room for mercy. Nowadays more than ever, there's no room for anything but the best. They need the best they can get to stay on top, and it sucks if things don't work out, but just because they don't, you can't expect someone to give you a pass for that. I mean, business has got to keep the business going without weak links sinking them, right?"

Alison thought about everything before she gave a somber nod. Carlos smirked before he patted her on the back. "So, no one can say I didn't try, Hector did say he could use an extra crewman. I'll make a call, if they like what your guy can do, it's on him, okay?"

"Thanks Carlos."

"No matter what I'll tell him he won't hear anything till we are done with this place, okay? Don't want him to drag things down while we are here."

"Thanks, makes sense."

"Just stand firm, Alison," Cammy said with a detached tone. "The sap is so hungry, just any breadcrumb of hope will keep him at bay till it's done. Then you can leave him forever to think about how foolish he was. Sounds like the bloke won't be able to do much about it but cry to his online echo chamber."

Alison thought about how anxious Kevin was every time he asked something. "Parts of what you say might be true, but seriously, Kevin knows not to get overconfident, Cammy. He's...been rejected so many times that he was anxious to ask me anything. He did not outright say it, but he's seen rejection so much, he's nervous to hope for anything good."

"Oh well, a spoiled man that keeps thinking he's entitled to things working out in his way could use a harsh reality check. He can love you all he wants, but no matter how sincere that love is, the harsh truth is that love is worthless if it comes from a person who's worthless. C'mon Alison, let's leave theses outdated obsolete men in the dust. As they fall, *we* rise."

As Cammy stormed out, Carlos chuckled. "Well, not sure I would put it like she did, but winners do take the spoils. Speaking of that, time to call Ernie to let him know the daily spoils. See you bright and early, chicas!"

As Carlos and most of the others left, Alison mumbled. "Kevin, I did what I could, the rest is up to you, and how in tune you are with reality."

With her purse and all inside it secure, Alison prepared to clear out before a disgruntled female voice cut in from the right. "That's right, just blame it all on everyone to feel good about yourself Ali. Glad to see you really are the same after a decade."

Alison froze and turned around to see who threw out that verbal jab. But it was not Cammy or any of her other co-workers, but a red-haired woman in a waitress outfit. Cammy saw the woman had short hair and just raised an eyebrow. "Sorry, do I know you? I'm sorry if you're confused about things miss, but I don't know you and I don't have time for random drunken rants."

"I know I've changed a bit since I'm not forcing it as much as you, Ali, but thought you would remember your old best bud Marge just a little bit, huh?"

Alison looked at the woman closely before she widened her eyes in shock. "My God, Marge, that's really you? I'm... I'm so sorry I didn't realize it was you this whole time! I—it's just it's been a while and you..."

"Yeah, I know I got a few extra pounds alright? *You* have twins and see how well *you* rebound, huh Ali? Lucky for me my entire existence does not revolve around how high petty jackasses rate me online, am I right? That's the thing about getting hitched and letting yourself go. Long as it's not to the point where you're unhealthy, it's kind of nice to be free of it. Though guess you focused on being free of other things, huh pal?"

Alison took a deep sigh before she leaned back. "I'm sorry you see things that way, Marge. It's been a while since we talked, but I would have hoped you would not have such a distorted view of things."

"They really get you to spew out one speech after another in your school, huh Ali? No need for all that professional talk when we used to be tight, right? Though, maybe it's just me 'distorting' things, but I remember you breaking away from me like a bad rash the last year you were around before ditching the state entirely! I'm not like Kevin, starving for attention from a woman that I'll let *anything* slide, you know!"

"Marge, I know I upset you when I left town, but after my parents' divorce, I had to!"

"Oh, don't give me that crap! People get some wiggle room but just because something bad happens to you, it does not give you a license to get out of whatever dick moves you make! I mean, no matter how hard it is to move, not even coming back for your own mom's funeral is just, really low."

Alison paused before she looked down. "You weren't there, alright Marge? I am sorry she was dying of cancer alone for months, but she was not there for me, she can't just try and forget all the harm she did just because she was desperate."

"Damn, that's cold Alison…real cold, since you treated everyone you knew here like they all were in on how your mom acted."

"I'm sorry we did not keep in touch, but nothing lasts forever, Marge! I more or less moved on to a different life after I left

Springfield!"

"Oh, come on, you think I don't know how the world works? Think I'm someone who lives in a living soap opera like you, Ali? I know things don't last forever, but what pissed me off is that you *never* said you were sorry."

"Is that what you wanted me to say? Then I'm sorry my actions hurt you Marge."

"Damn it, say it like you *mean* it! But you're not sorry, I can see it in your face. You're so much of a big shot that you're just stopping by to throw a few scraps to those you left behind before becoming a bigger shot, huh?"

"Are you really acting this way because you're jealous, Marge? I'm sorry if I hurt you, but I'm not sorry if I'm doing better than you."

"Oh please, you think I *want* your life? You may be living the life now Alison, but no matter how good a game you got, it's a short ride and it really sucks when you have to get off! I may not have seen as much as you have riding around showing off all over everywhere, but I've seen enough in this and the other places I bar tended.

I've seen plenty of gals, and guys for that matter, try and hang on to their 'prime years' like they were holding on to dear life, because for some of them it is their life because they did not think things through! I don't care if you listen to me or not, Alison, but every dream ends sooner or later, so are you still going to have a cute little blog or gonna be another lady that goes dark on the web after you're no longer in the top ten?"

"I'm *well* aware nothing lasts forever, Marge," Alison retorted coolly. "I have been trying to secure things so that I'm in a firm place once things need to change."

"Oh, got your own plans that you're so sure will come true, huh? Guess you and Kevin have more in common than I thought. Even back then he adored the hell out of you. Just like then, you could get him to do anything you wanted. Somethings never change."

Alison paused as she thought about all Kevin had said to her since the two had caught up before flicking her hair back. "Maybe a little, but I seem to have thought out my plans a bit better than he has at the moment. Still, it's not like that. I remember, me and Kevin became friends after another kid dared him to kiss that Mary girl, and her older sister beat him up after school.

We were assigned on the same class project by chance after that, and he was to afraid to talk to me. Still, I promised if he did not do anything rude to me, I would not do anything rude to him, and, we were friends after that. I never meant to harm him, I just had to do what I needed to do in order to move on. I am not sure Kevin has pushed himself as hard yet.

Maybe I was just luckier that the economy was favorable for what I was good at compared to Kevin, but that's how life goes at times. I truly do want Kevin to have a good life, but he needs to see what's real and work to what he can get before it's too late."

"Ha, big words for someone who all but forgot he was alive just a few days ago, huh Ali? Me and Kevin have hardly talked much the past few years. Being a family gal, we hardly are in the same circles, not to mention I don't really like the same stuff he likes. Still, we are friends on Facebook, so I see the gist of what he's up to when I'm bored on dull nights. It's not that great, to be honest, but at least he's still staying afloat, however desperately. Alison, Kevin may not be doing that great, but he's hanging on.

You were not friends with some of them but some of our classmates just snapped completely, gave up, are now nothing but deadbeat drunks or worse. Not all of them wanted to be like that, but they got screwed over and just broke down because the world had nothing for them. Hell, I think one guy we used to know snapped so bad he killed his parents and is spending the rest of his life at Ratched

Falls.

Kevin at least is still not giving up on living. I'm not going to swoon over him for that, but at least I can respect him."

"And I respect him for that too, Marge, but that does not change what I need."

"I did not say you needed him. Playing matchmaker is too much of a pain for me. When I'm not getting paid for it at least. I'm just saying, don't feel too much better than the rest of us. It really was just luck, you're not as special as you think you are."

"Well, if that's how you feel, Marge, then so be it. I see a lot has changed, if you would like I would be happy to catch up with you for an hour or so."

"Oh, now you have time to spare, huh? I'm not too close to Kevin, but I'm not big on serving two-faced stuck ups, either, when they are this crappy with hiding it."

"Don't be like that Marge, I have a boyfriend. I can't give Kevin the wrong idea!"

"Oh, you have a boyfriend that you don't even feel like talking about to make things clear?"

"Well, we are not an official couple yet, but it's close enough. You know things are not as simple as we wish."

"Only if you keep trying to make things messy, Doll face."

"Seriously? If you're going to be this petty, I might be forced to leave a harsh review online."

"Ha, that's the best you got? You thought you guys were so merciful to grace this place with your presence, but because it's so rare I'll get more bragging rights for sticking it up to the elite. Face it, Alison, you're not as big a deal as you thought you were. Fact, you're so not a big deal. I'm going home because I'd rather check in on my kids than waste time with a faker. Unless you manage to become the next Anne Hathaway or something, have fun on the ride while it lasts Alison. Oh, and tell Teri she's bringing the drinks next time. I'm still cool with her, even if you piss me off."

Marge walked back into the office, leaving Alison alone. She took a few moments to gather her thoughts before she quickly walked out of the Frosty Penguin. As she struggled not to let her frustration show, she grasped her phone tightly.

Damn it Marge, all this time and she has to be so petty? I'm sorry if things did not work out how she wanted them to but she didn't have to be that petty about it. I didn't want to hurt her, Kevin, or anyone else but I did what I had to in order to not fall behind.

Life's not fair but losing just to stay behind with everyone is not fun, either. I know I can't live like this forever, but that's why I have to secure things so that when things do have to change, I can cash in.

Alison was about to unlock her car when she saw she got a text from Chandler. As she laughed at his joke and thought about all she had done to get this far before, her expression stiffened.

It's impossible for everyone to be happy, so I just got to find a way to climb as high as I can without crushing too many in my way. Kevin, Marge, I don't want to hurt you guys or anyone else. But someone always gets hurt, so I just have to make sure it's not for no reason. Kevin, I don't want to hurt you but it's up to you to be able to see things clearly. Well, I'll see.

8

The Weight of Blood

Even if things did not go *completely* according to plan, Kevin was happy that it seemed like he was able to hold his own with Alison's co-workers. He was even more motivated to leave a good impression so that Carlos and the others would give him a good recommendation to increase the odds he could leave a good impression on Alison.

And so, after getting the stuff Bart wanted and hanging out for a bit, Kevin quickly went on to the next filming event with Starlight.

To go with the overall theme of the town's history, the theme of the day was during the era of the Great Depression. This was another important part of the town's history as the people of that time endured a rough period that broke some of the surrounding towns, thanks to coming together, Springfield was able to hang on and rebound stronger than before.

With a few modifications, Alison, Cammy, and the rest of the Starlight models were able to show their individual spin on each outfit to make it a cover shot, at least in Kevin's eyes.

Kevin worked with Sam to get everyone's good side, but as he tried to give a wide shot of Alison while she was posing, Bright walked over and cleared his throat. "What you doing still focusing on that girl, Kevin? At this rate we are going to have enough stock footage to fill in for all the events of the year."

While Bright was whispering, Kevin could tell from his look it was not meant as a joke before he gave an uneasy chuckle. "Hey Bright. I know I'm lingering a bit, but I swear I know what I'm doing. See, I got an idea to have it focus on her for a bit while showing a picture of someone from the time period where I would talk about the history."

"Oh, another attempt at trying to turn *my* stuff into something for the History Channel, Kevin? I thought I told you the audience we have does not turn to our channel for history, but just to see the local events or news!"

"I know that's true, but I just had an idea that could cover both areas at once and with the right editing it could come off as…"

"As *not* what I wanted," Bright said bluntly. He put his arm over Kevin's shoulder before he smirked. "Just remember kid, do I pay you for ideas or for being an assistant to do what I *want* on the shoot?"

Kevin was about to say Bright was not paying him at all before he remembered the rant the older man went on last time about the value of "experience," causing him to wince. "You're right, sorry Bright, I'll just do what you want."

"Now that's the sound of a good worker, kid! Speaking of being a good worker, how about letting me take over? We got some boys from the Visual Audio Connections coming in to lend a hand for some special lighting, all for that vintage feel and all. How about helping them set up while I cover? The faster this goes, the more work we get done."

"Of course, Bright, I'm on it. Wait, which group you say it was? That nearly sounds like…"

"God damn it kid, all that matters is that *I* want you to help them!"

"Of course, sorry."

Kevin glanced to the right, saw Alison was too busy posing to notice him and went over to where a van was arriving. As people stepped out of the van, Kevin recognized one of them, the tall man with red hair and a beard in glasses was one of his friends since high school.

As the man walked towards him while talking to two others in the same uniform, Kevin walked up to him while waving. "Hey Guile! Good to see ya, man! Didn't know you were going to be helping us out today. Hell, didn't think you guys would be here today!"

Guile paused before he nodded at his co-workers. He readjusted his glasses as he walked up to Kevin curiously. "Kevin? To be honest didn't think you would be here either. I thought you were substitute teaching these days, man?"

"Yeah, I am, but I take days off every now and then to help Bright and the others out. Besides with more of the schools closed…less jobs and all. But, it gives me more time to focus on getting things to kick off here. After all, I want to keep things going on as many things as I can.

"Still trying to have it all when you got nothing, huh buddy? Well, that's your choice, man. Bright has a deal with some of the top brass in VAC so here we are. So…you know what's going on, man?"

"Yeah, you need help setting up the lights and stuff?"

"More or less. Thanks."

"No problem Guile, want to see this go as smooth as possible, you know? Just wish you told me so I could have planned things out more and all."

"It's fine man, I mean, after all, you don't really have a say in much of how it goes down, right?"

"Er…right about the big projects like this, I guess. Still, just meant that there is more to this than a job to me. You remember Alison, Guile? Ah, my friend that was around for the first half of high school? I talked about her a lot back then."

"You talked about a lot of girls, Kevin," Guile said with restrained annoyance. "No offense man, but we have a job to do, don't have time to waste on you talking about another girl that ended up being another fake friend trolling you, man."

Kevin winced as he saw Guile's co-workers snicker before he cleared his throat. "This is not a fake girl, Guile, Alison's someone I knew even before you! She's right over there!"

He pointed to Alison, who was walking back to get a water bottle and saw Kevin before she winked at him.

Guile saw it to before he sighed. "Well, she does look sort of familiar. So, you're here to try and make her shoot look good to impress her or something, man?"

"Well, I mean just helping out, but if she likes how it comes out then, that would be a nice bonus, right?"

"Kevin…nothing's wrong with doing a good job, but remember how you were all excited trying to impress that girl you met on that dating site what, six years ago and after we had that good time in the city you thought you impressed her, and you never heard from her again?"

Kevin had bitter memories as he remembered how the woman, he talked with the most on a dating site got his hopes up, only to crush them when she vanished without a word.

He clenched his fist tightly as he tried to give a casual shrug. "Alison is *not* like Nina, Guile. She's someone I know, a real friend, not just someone who is stringing me along for laughs. That's why I want to try and make sure things go as good as possible for her while she's here."

"All right, I get it man. But if you want to do that, Kevin, help me get the lights set up on time so we don't run behind schedule."

"Got it man. Awesome, just like old times!"

"Not quite Kevin, after all at least *I'm* getting paid, if things go well and all."

Kevin saw Guile had a joking tone in his voice and tried to not take his remark as an insult before he just nodded. Although Kevin had a few hiccups putting things together, he was able to fix them before Guile, Bright, Carlos, or any of the other people in a higher position than him could get annoyed.

While the models were taking breaks or making adjustments, Kevin managed to catch up a bit with Guile and hear how his wife was doing with her new job and how his newborn kid was doing. Before Kevin knew it, the shoot was completed.

Carlos saw Alison and the others looked relieved before he laughed. "Way to nail it, chicas! Only one more phase to go, and it's time to say adios to Alison's hometown! Thanks for making things flow smoothly, Bright."

"Just doing my job as a professional, Carlos," Bright answered before the two shook hands. "Maybe, but always a pleasure to work with someone who takes his work seriously. Thanks to how well you guys have handled things we are on the home stretch already."

"Always find it more profitable to be ahead of schedule. Long as things stay on track should be smooth sailing, Carlos."

"Should be, though some more of the bigger fish are coming in to bring some final adjustments for the last part. Shouldn't be too big, it's just that the final part is the one they use for all the promotions on TV and online, so they want to trim it up to be extra stylish, ya know what I mean?"

"Loud and clear, kid. Trust me, I used to work with serious companies all the time with bosses that loved to micromanage to make themselves feel better. Just keep me in the loop and it will be just fine."

"Sounds good, Sir. Right now, the plan is to take a break because everyone here sure as hell deserves it."

Kevin gave a sigh of relief and smiled at getting the job done right. But it dawned on him that there was a good chance his time with Alison was coming to an end unless something happened. "Damn, talk about time flying by when you're having fun. Only a little bit of time left to work on this. Got to make sure it goes right to get the right results."

Guile chuckled before he checked his phone. "Well, that's the job, right, buddy? I know you like to think ahead and dream big, Kevin, but just make sure you focus on getting the job done right before anything else. Well, was a fun bonus catching up with you man, but I better get going."

Kevin raised an eyebrow as he looked around. "Oh, you have to leave so soon, Guile? I mean, if you have time want to catch up more over lunch?"

"Sorry Kevin, got more work to do. Maybe another time."

Kevin heard Guile's co-workers talk about getting lunch before he cleared his throat. "Oh, got another job right after, huh man? Damn, your place works you ragged all right. It just sounds like your co-workers are going to lunch."

Guile took a deep breath before he glanced at Kevin with a careful look. "That's true man, but they don't have *my* responsibilities. Besides, I don't just have work stuff to handle but stuff a father has to take care of to. C'mon Kevin, thought I made it clear by now that there is a lot more to a real job that has real responsibilities compared to an entry level job that's supposed to only be a starting role."

Kevin saw Guile was overall friendly but had a tinge of annoyance in his eyes before he winced and looked down. "Sorry Guile, didn't mean to get in the way of your work or your kid or anything. Of course, it's fine if you're busy. But maybe we can plan out a dinner or something later in the week? Or, next week? I mean, if it's till the holidays, I'm fine."

"I'll see Kevin, but you know by now how busy things are for me, so I hope you're still reasonable about it and don't really think we have the time we had in high school and college. Some of us have more to do after work now, after all."

"Of course, Guile. I know you have a lot going on and all. It's just, hanging out one weekend a month, that's not asking too much is it? I mean, that's what friends do, right?"

"Kevin, don't take this the wrong way but you still let TV shape your expectations. Despite what *Seinfeld, Friends, Cheers, How I Met Your Mother* and all those other sitcoms led us all to believe, even close friends don't have the time to have dinner and talk every night about their day, or even every week. Even if that's how things used to be, it's just too damn expensive to go out every night. Don't take this the wrong way man, I still see you as a friend and all, but to be honest, with how little free time I have these days, I need to spend it on things that are new. That's why, if you have nothing new to say then there's really no point to spending time on what can be talked about with a text, right? The sad truth, Kevin, is that these days personal time is an investment."

"Well, I mean there is all kinds of new stuff to talk about, Guile! I mean on Netflix the new season of..."

"C'mon Kevin, to be honest if I care about someone's views on a season of a show or a new movie or a video game I would go listen to a podcast. I'm talking about what is new personally from *you?*"

Kevin looked uneasy as he tried to keep his composure and chuckled uneasily. "Well c'mon man, you know it's hard to gain momentum these days. But I mean I applied to a few more sites to be a voice actor and all."

"Yeah…and?"

"And…that's it because I have not heard from them, a month later. But I did hear back from that one friend of my mom's dad's friend's friend who knew about my grandfather for the documentary I've been trying to get together."

"And?"

"And, they have not gotten back to me. But I *did* hear from the job at the school."

"Yeah…*and?*"

"And…she said she found a teacher that fit her personal style more, and had more experience, but that I should keep trying, but did not respond when I asked for more feedback."

"So, you *really* are nowhere closer at all?"

"Well I mean, Bright and Sam keep saying they are impressed with my guts and that they might have an opening soon."

"Kevin, no offense but they said that years ago, right?"

Kevin made sure his bosses were not too close before he gave a weak smile to try and mask his dismay. "I know Guile, trust me, I know. But what else can I do? How was I supposed to know all those people were just lying to me and just leave when I thought I was going to get to the part where I made money? How was I supposed to know as soon as I got a job at the radio station, they were going to replace DJ's with robot jockeys? How was I supposed to know all that time trying to get a job at the county college would amount to nothing because they would close without warning anyone? There have been a lot of setbacks, no doubt there. Still, hanging on till I make it, it's the American Dream, right? I mean, it's not like I don't send resumes, but what am I supposed to do when I don't hear back from anyone? You know what it's like spending years sending out resumes, and only hear back from a handful of them, only to not get hired by *any* of them?"

Kevin saw Guile close his eyes for a moment before Guile sighed. "Ever think about looking in different areas, man? You're right that making your dream come true is the American Dream, but maybe we all have to realize for most of us it's the American Mirage at this point? And, the American *Reality* is that there is a lot less stuff to go around than we were all told.

Not like I'm happy about it either, but the truth is that because of what people our parents age did, most of us will *never* be able to have it as easy as they had it, for anything. Truthfully, we might very well see our standard of living be reduced to how it was over a century ago.

We won't have houses as big as them, we won't be able to have the jobs that people somehow liked having, and all in all we will have to work harder for less. You think I like having to scramble from one job to another just to keep my house?

Not one bit, but I know trying to rage like I'm Batman or Daredevil or something won't change anything, that's not how the real world works man. As much as we all got screwed over, there is a good chance there is nothing any of us can do with it but deal.

So, we must take what we can get or get nothing, but just dreaming for a kind of life that does not exist anymore won't do anything. Let's face it, Kevin, you're already thirty. Maybe it's time to try focusing on something else?"

"How is that going to work, Guile? If I can't break through on the things I'm most passionate about, how am I going to do well in things I'm not as good at?"

"Because if you want to live Kevin, you don't really have a choice but to figure something out. Maybe you can't be a superstar, but you will live. Maybe you will never be able to afford your own place and always need roommates to afford a place, but you will get used to it if you try and settle with what is real. You think my dream was to just mostly do tech work where I have to work so many hours, I hardly see my family?

Not a chance, but it's the only way to pay the bills, and being able to live is something. Kevin, don't take this the wrong way, but maybe it's time you focus on what you can really do to live in the world as it is? You clearly have not been able to break out into acting, film, or any of that. Maybe you could have at one point, but the fact is the bar's just too high for someone like you to make it. Maybe it's time to think that maybe it's because it's not a fit for you?"

"What? Come on, Guile, don't be like that. We both talked about all the actors and all kinds of stars who took decades to break in. I just have to keep looking and find a way to seize that damn light at the end of the tunnel. It's just not easy when you don't have any connections to break through and all. I mean, even you got your job because of someone your mom knew, right?"

"That's true Kevin. Still, it's a lot easier if you're looking for what really fits. Ever think you're not fit for these kinds of roles? Maybe something lower key, and something you can manage with less pressure?"

"C'mon Guile, we both know programming stuff's not my expertise. How am I supposed to make a living off of clerk work or something?"

"You can if you're reasonable man. It's no dream life, but it's *a* life. Hell, you might even have to move to another state but it's still a life."

"Another state? Guile, I'm *barely* been hanging on as it is, it would be all that much harder keeping things together somewhere where I would not know anyone."

"That's the thing Kevin, you're always putting off the difficult stuff for the short-term comfort. If you could keep a job and the pay was enough to live on, you could work the rest of the stuff out. I know it's not as simple as that Kevin, but please, take this from a friend, not wanting you to use up the rest of your life going nowhere because you would not compromise.

If you're not willing to seriously try and do whatever it takes and your life just keeps ending up being about the same old stuff then well, I'll still be there for you when you and your family need me. However, I hope you can understand why I don't have time for the same old same old. I do enjoy our talks, but talking to anyone who just goes on about how the world should be just gets tiring."

Kevin paused for a moment and grit his teeth as he tried to not let his feelings run wild. "Guile, you really think I'm just goofing around here? I worked to get my Masters *and* Doctorate damn it, I pushed as hard as I could!"

"I know you worked hard man, but while I think that's impressive, the sad truth is that even a Doctorate or whatever don't mean much if it's not the right field these days. After how bad times have gotten, there are only a few places where someone can thrive. You really have to look at what the world wants instead of just spending years waiting for the dream job to pop up."

"I know I play more video games than you these days but damn it, that's because for a while now it's the *only* time I feel like I'm winning at all. You know how depressing it feels at times when the only time you feel like you can win, is in a dream world? It's not like I've been having it easy, for god's sake I did not want to waste your time with trivial stuff, but it really hurt when you were not around when my mom had cancer.

My dad was stressed, my mom was sick, and I had to keep doing stuff to keep things together. You think that was fun and games for me? You know how stressful it was when just as I thought I was about to get up, the world seemed like it collapsed?"

"No, and I'm sorry I was not around more when you were stressed out about that man," Guile said patiently. "I have to do what it takes to keep my job too, you know. Look man, I know you're not happy where you are, and you want to go places. It's not that I think you're not trying, it's just that you can't spend your life doing the same thing and expecting different results. Just focus on finding a place, *any* place where you can grow, even if it's not what you thought your life would be. That's more important before anything else, even love."

"Why…you think no one will love me as I am now?"

"Kevin…I'd be lying if I say it never happens, but the less reasons people have to have faith in you does not help. Just tell me, you have any idea at all if this friend of yours sees you any more than that Nina girl that you said liked you that time we were at the park before she ghosted you? I know you were friends with her in school but what does that mean now?"

Kevin looked conflicted as he realized he had trouble thinking of the answer. As he tried to think of something, suddenly Alison walked up from the right to throw out a casual, "Hey Kevin!"

Kevin turned around to see Alison walking up to the two with a friendly wave. As Kevin waved back, Alison smirked. "Great job again today. Sounds like you were doing double duty, huh? Is this one of your co-workers?"

Kevin saw Alison looked sincere before he chuckled. "Not quite, more like an old friend. This is Guile Nash, I met him right around the time you left."

Alison saw Guile look at her carefully before she shrugged. "Guile? Sorry, I can't seem to remember your face."

"It's alright, I don't really look like how I looked in high school and we were not really in the same circles. Still, you're Alison Winters, the friend Kevin had before we started hanging out? It's a pleasure to meet you."

"Same here."

Kevin saw his two friends shake hands before Guile looked back at Kevin. "So, I heard you two have been catching up and making up for lost time last night?"

"Oh, you mean at the Frosty Penguin? Well, even if he's not a member of Starlight, he helped us, so it felt right to include him in the after party. I admit we don't have anything set yet, but you guys are welcome to the next party we have."

"Thanks, but have to check with my wife before I commit to anything," Guile answered. "Speaking of that, don't mean to be rude but I have to get going now. Got about ten things to do before I can call it a day."

"I understand," Alison threw out playfully. "Got twenty more things to do before the day ends and I have to add another thirty on the list. But that's just keeping a job these days, right? It was a pleasure to meet you, Guile."

"Thanks, you too, Alison. Kevin, sorry we didn't have too much time to hang out, but I'll see how things look in the next few weeks, okay? That's all I can do, but I promise I will try and see if there will be a spot open sometime this month."

"Thanks man," Kevin responded gratefully. "That's all I ask. Well, say hi to the family for me."

"Will do."

Kevin went for a handshake, but Guile patted him on the shoulder before walking out. Alison smiled as he walked out, "I didn't know you had other friends in this job of yours, Kevin. Glad you have co-workers your age to work with."

"Well, he's going all over the country for jobs, so we don't have as much time to hang out as I would have liked. He travels so often and still doesn't get paid as much as you would think for all that."

"I know how he feels about feeling underappreciated at times, but we've got to do what we can to get noticed and celebrate the victories we can get, right?"

"You got it Alison. Do you know what you guys are doing

tonight?"

"Not yet, was just about to ask Cammy. I have to take care of a few things, but if you don't mind waiting, I can let you know before you leave."

"Sure, thanks."

Alison winked before going off and Kevin smiled. He looked at where Guile's van was parked, but saw his friend was already left.

Guile's a lot further ahead in life than I am, and I know he's right about a lot of things. But I can't just give up, otherwise all the years I spent, would have been for nothing, and I'll end up like my dad's brother or my mom's sister, miserable and just spend the rest of life on autopilot, alone. Alison seems like she wants to hang out with me, she's a real friend. I just have to not blow it and…

Before he could finish his thought Kevin's phone started ringing. He saw it was his dad and raised an eyebrow before he quickly answered it. "Dad, what is it? I'm still at work."

"I know that boy, this is *after* work. Don't make any plans for movies or nothing, we are going out to dinner for an early birthday celebration."

"What the hell, you like going out to dinner all of a sudden?"

"It's a time Bart, your Uncle and my pal Chuck can all make it, so we are moving it up! I'm doing it for you, Kevin, so Bart can be there too! You're the one always moaning about how you hate just being stuck with my brother and Chuck at your stuff!

"Damn it boy, like you have anything else going on besides playing video games or watching shows when you get back anyway."

"Still think that way about what I do, Dad? Damn it, I write and work on stuff, but you just *never* pay attention! Besides, I might have something planned with Alison."

"What, a date?"

"Well, no but she might be doing something."

"Damn it Kevin, it's one thing if you were doing something, but you're not holding up things for damn wishes again! You are a part of this family, boy, so you will do what the head of the family wants so quit moaning! And bring more drinks on the way home, Bart drank the rest of the wine after he got back from his night job and I want something for my celebration."

Kevin's father hung up before he could even argue, causing him to take a deep breath as he put his phone back.

Damn it, I wasn't looking forward to being stuck around another one of my dad's drinking sessions. Hopefully, he won't go to overboard with mom around.

Kevin's thoughts were cut off as Alison returned with a sheepish grin. "Hey Kevin, sorry but we are not sure what's going on yet tonight. A few people haven't decided as yet, but we might know in a few hours."

Kevin winced as he thought about how many ways his dad could mess things up before he sighed. "Thanks for that Alison. But if it's in the evening I might not be able to make it. My dad's going to have his birthday dinner tonight. To be honest I would not hesitate to go with whatever you guys are doing, but I know if I don't go, he won't let me hear the end of it for like, the rest of the year. Sorry, I know that's kind of lame."

Alison saw Kevin looked ashamed before she smirked. "It's fine Kevin, not like we have anything planned yet anyway. Trust me, I know how valuable family time is when it can be so fragile. Don't worry about it, not like this is the end or anything. We will just have to make the next time even more awesome, right?"

"There *is* gonna be another time, right?"

Alison saw Kevin looked worried before she smiled. "Of course, silly. Not like we will just pack up and leave."

"Thanks Alison, I'll make sure that I have everything ready for…"

Before he could go on Sam walked up suddenly and yelled, "Hey Kevin! Are you going to help us pack up or what? You didn't think just because your pal left you were done, did you?"

Kevin saw Bright and Carlos looking at him in the distance before he chuckled anxiously. "Oh of course not Sam. Just was trying to…"

"C'mon man, did not seem like you were trying to pack a camera away to me and that's *all* that matters!"

"Right. Sorry Alison, better wrap things up here."

"It's fine. Hang in there Kevin, I'll reach out to you soon."

Kevin hurried off to put the tripod away and Alison waved as she left, Kevin realized that he hadn't thanked her before she left.

I guess Kevin isn't the only one being called out, and I'm starting to guess it's from all sides. Geez, I don't want people to think I'm his girlfriend but don't want people to think he was just imagining we are friends either. I mean, after what Marge said and after what he told me, I can see it's not like he's not trying. I know what it's like to keep getting turned down, in other areas at least. At this point I think it's clear another person telling him he's not where he should be would not really help anyone.

I really do wish I could help him somehow. I guess most of it will come down to what he's willing to do to get things to change. Still, maybe if I could find the right way to push him in the right direction before I leave, a way without making him feel ashamed or overwhelmed. I know I had to feel safe before I had the nerve to make changes.

Her thought was cut off as a male chuckle caught her attention, followed up with a slick, "What's the matter, babe? It's a crime for such a superstar to be frowning!"

Alison was shocked as she turned around and saw a man in a slick black jacket with a crisp navy-blue shirt stroll up. He had gelled back hair and sunglasses. He flashed a wide camera-friendly grin, she couldn't help but giggle in excitement. "Chandler! You're here!"

"Course I am, doll, would be rather damn embarrassing if I was in Australia now?"

Chandler picked Alison up and hugged her. "Sorry you were stuck for so long alone in dingy memory lane Ali, but business before pleasure, right? But I got it all out of the way so we can wrap things up here and have a game changing experience in Paris!"

"Oh wow, you really were able to pull that off?"

"Do you know who you're talking to, Ali? Girl, have you been drinking? Cause that's the only reason I could understand why you'd think I don't put my money where my mouth is, babe. It's all like we talked about. You will win over the cream of the fashion crop and get to where you deserve to be, love. Then I can say I'm dating a superstar."

"Chandler...thank you," Alison said happily before she kissed him passionately. She got lost in the kiss it was as if she was in her own world, she reluctantly broke away from him. Chandler winked. "Course love. Figured you deserved something after having to put up with this stroll down memory lane. Though between what you and Carlos told me, sounds like you had plenty of local help making sure things ran smoothly, huh? Sounds like many did not realize they let a diamond escape from their grasp and only realized they pushed away one of the few good things they had after the fact."

Alison saw how dismissive Chandler was of her hometown before she said. "Oh, don't be that way, Chandler. I know I ranted a few times about all the reasons I wanted to get away, but even if it's down on its luck somewhat, it's still far from a horrible place."

"True Ali, I mean any place that you lived in can't be beyond redemption. And, I did already scope out a place that is fitting enough for us to have dinner. You didn't try out the place here called Ruby right? It has passable food and a bar with staff good enough to serve people of our calibre."

"Is that so? So is that where we are going to have tonight's party?"

"Carlos has other plans, because this is just for you and me, love. Much as I'm eager to get the lowdown from Cammy and the others about their take here, I think the gal I'm fond of the most deserves the most time. There will be time for the rest later. I think it's a capital idea to make up for lost time, don't you think?"

"Chandler, that's so sweet. Thank you."

"Oh, that's just part of our entire reunion menu, Alison. But before we begin with the appetizer, just how are things going? Getting what you wanted from this?"

Alison thought of her time over the past few days and thought about Kevin before she blushed and looked down. "It's been fun getting in touch with my past to get a better grasp on what I want for the future. Got me to remember some parts of myself."

"Well I'll love meeting *all* parts of you by the end of the night. Just got to wrap up the usual red tape and we won't have anyone from your past in the way of our future, Ali."

"Sounds good Chandler, looks like tonight just might be magical."

"I do have that touch, babe, just wait and see."

As Alison giggled in anticipation, Chandler went on to catch up with the rest of her co-workers to clear the way for good times. Alison was grateful Kevin left before he saw her with Chandler so she could avoid this moment being ruined by a possible awkward exchange. Luckily for her, as soon as Kevin finished putting away the rest of the gear for Bright, he went home.

***

After doing some chores and some writing for his novel, Kevin hung out with Bart before he reluctantly went to dinner with his parents. The place they ended up for dinner was Ruby's.

Kevin's group ran into his dad's brother Jack and best friend Chuck, and with the two additional middle-aged balding men, sat at the table reserved for them.

Kevin was quickly relieved the table was in a corner as his dad started drinking before they even got appetizers. Kevin told Bart about his day, but Bart soon started drinking and Kevin was left mostly to himself, thinking of ways to impress Alison.

By the time the main course had arrived, Bart slapped him in the back and knocked him out of his trance. As he snapped to attention, Bart just laughed. "Damn bro, you missed my joke! What the hell are you daydreaming about now?"

"Oh, sorry man. Just thinking of some ideas for work and all that. If that Carlos can come through for me, maybe I can get a break."

"That's all, man? You're not still dreaming of winning over that chick?"

As Bart laughed loudly, Kevin got defensive. "C'mon Bart, have at least a little faith will ya? She was impressed with how I was last time. If I can just do well for the rest of the event, just maybe I can."

"Can *what* boy?" Kevin's father grunted from the edge of the table. "Spend money for a girl that will just string you along before you're back to square one with *less* money?"

"Oh, come on dad, you're the one who keeps nagging me to take more risks and now you're not happy when I do it? It's because you're such a damn hypocrite that I've had so many mixed signals over the years!"

"Don't blame me, Kevin, you refuse to listen to what I'm really trying to say! I want you to take action, but also be smart about it. No matter how much you and Alison played together when you were kids, it's clear she's now someone that is not anywhere close to the same area as you!"

"Damn it, real supportive dad, telling your son he's out of his league."

"Better to set you straight before it blows up in your face again!

All I'm saying is that a girl like Alison is looking for something you don't got. If you were a bit more realistic about what is suited for you in a girl, maybe you would not have wasted so many years on pipe dreams!"

"I'm not just going to fall in love with someone I'm not attracted to, dad! How would you have felt if someone told you who you should have married?"

"There is a difference between being told and seeing what's right boy! Me and your mother were set up by friends, and while it was not love at first sight, we realized we were fit for each other!"

Kevin's mother just sipped on the drink she was having before she shrugged. "True about it not being a love first sight thing, dear. I guess, after seeing how things were going in life it felt right and I guess you did make me laugh, at the time."

Kevin saw his mom looking detached before he grimaced. "I have nothing against being set up with friends if they are serious about it, dad. Hell, I'd love that, but it seems hard to find time to pull that off these days."

Bart saw Kevin glance at him before he shrugged. "Sorry bro, but my job comes first before helping you score. But you're trying *too* hard Kevin. Your dad's right that instead of pushing too much you got to be natural about it."

"See, you listen to Bart, boy!" Biff slurred out. "Just do what your old man tells you to do already! After things failed enough, figured you would be keen on changing the game plan, huh?"

"Your bright ideas? Like you insisting that taking that gym class in the city will get me a date? Damn it, dad, I talked to more than a few people I know, and they *all* said that women don't like being approached at the gym and they are all women so they *might* know something about it!"

"Bah, I'm your father! My word means more than a few strangers or co-workers!"

"One of the people who told me that was your sister!"

"I love her, but she is not the best expert on dating."

"Your dad's right, Kevin," Chuck slurred out. "You've got to show some guts to win over the ladies! I mean, it worked for me once, twenty years ago. Just too bad she ended up being two-faced. But you've got to take risks before you run out of time and hair. Trust me, it's a lot harder without the hair."

Kevin saw his uncle shrug before he chugged his drink down. "Oh, don't be too hard on him, guys. Some guys are just not meant to have a relationship. Don't worry too much, Kevin, trust me, sometimes the single life is better, makes things a lot simpler. If I had a relationship, it would have got in the way of taking care of ma all those years!"

Kevin saw how hollow his uncle's eyes were before he cleared his throat. "Uncle Jack, you really were fine not having anyone but aides as you spent a decade living with Grandma?"

"My mother needed me, Kevin, and I repaid all she did for me. Not like I missed out on anything anyway."

"See Kevin? That's how a good *grateful* son acts!" Biff said with a wide-eyed look. Kevin repressed shuddering in disgust in front of his uncle before he cleared his throat. "Ah, come on Uncle Jack, don't give up just because you turned sixty. I mean, I heard people in their seventies find true love."

"It's *not* for me, okay!?" Jack said with a sudden rageful outburst. As his eye twitched, he poured more wine into his glass. "I know what I want more than anyone Kevin, and I don't want to go through the damn cycle again! Some are meant to live with others, some are better alone."

Bart saw Jack's eye twitch before he snickered. "Don't feel like you have to defend yourself, Jack, some men are better off free without any baggage weighing them down. I wouldn't mind having a good gal around to make things fun, but I'm sure as hell not just going to chain myself to a dame just to have someone cook for me."

"Oh, come on dude, my mom's right there!"

"Ha, Momma Summers knows I'm not dissing her, Kevin, chill out. I'm just saying, I saw my brother get dragged down and lose half of everything because he ended up marrying someone who was not a good fit for him. Sometimes it's better to be lonely if it means having your freedom. Just got to be man enough to handle it.

You don't have the guts to live on your own, Kevin. Girls can see that, maybe before anything you have to man up before a girl will stick around. Prove you're a man that can handle life and maybe they will see you are man enough to date. On top of that maybe if you go for a girl that you have a shot with maybe it won't be such a joke."

"Damn it, maybe I'd have a little more confidence if the people closest to me had more faith in me. If you guys gave me more support, then maybe I could have made a breakthrough by now! If I had a better reputation, then it would be easier to impress…"

Kevin was cut off as his father broke into a burst of crude laughter. Kevin's father kept laughing as his face got red and puffy because of the wine.

He saw people looking at his dad and he used all of his will power to not shout at him. His dad kept laughing till he started coughing violently.

He was making a near whimpering-like cough for so long that the waiter came over. But Biff just put out his arm to pause him as he gave a wide crude smile. "You're past thirty and *still* have the same damn dreams you had from college, boy? I didn't want to make you even more moody, so I played along, but it's time you wake up while you still have a chance to act!

"Real life is not the movies, video games, and all the other stories you love so much, Kevin. Sure, we all love the stories about the good old American dream about the down on his luck bum who through sheer will power goes from rags to riches with old fashion grit! But the thing is son, is that they have skills that stand out! You have your talents, boy, and I'm proud of it, but the honest truth is that you're *not* a genius, or at least not in the things that most people care about.

"This is not a movie where you suddenly get a golden ticket, and everything changes one day. You're not going to become a superhero suddenly, Kevin, and unless a miracle happens, and you win the lottery or something you're not suddenly going to be a superstar. So, instead of spending time trying to be what you're not, just accept what you are and work with that. We are not a famous family Kevin, we are just an average bunch of people with average talents, and it will be damn tough for anyone who wants something more than average to pick you boy.

"Ducks stick with ducks and hawks stick with hawks. Ducks that try and mingle with hawks or swans or peacocks or whatever's not the same species as them are damn fools, so the only real thing a duck can do is stop dreaming a hawk or whatever will be with him and stick with its fellow duck, where it belongs!"

"Damn it, damn you dad!"

"What, you want me to lie to you till I die that you're something you're not? You're not secretly a superhero or anything, so be a man and accept what you are already! Just take what you can get before you don't get anything, boy!"

Kevin felt himself on the verge of being consumed with anger as he grasped the table tightly. "Damn it dad, I'm not giving up trying to change what I am, or who I can be, unlike you! You, you refused to change at all in like, ever. Even after you had a heart attack, even after things got worse and worse, you *never* change!"

"Because I'm not dancing to everyone's tune, boy!" Kevin's father roared furiously. "I'm done fooling myself! I am who I am, and everyone who has a problem with that can screw off!"

"You say that even though you have like, four friends at most!?"

"Who needs fake friends anyway, Kevin? Look at you, you keep trying to impress these people you don't know anything about just because they are important or cool? I just need people who understand me and enjoy me for what I am! Why bother kissing the ass of my bitch of a boss when my true pals here will go to that Turkish restaurant and enjoy every damn minute of it!"

At hearing that, Kevin saw his uncle wince before clearing his throat. "Well, guess you were too drunk to remember, Biff, but I did say last time I would prefer to eat at a place where I'm not allergic to half the stuff."

"Oh, you're just as picky as my son, Jack! It's the spirit of being with people who understand you! Because I don't want to be with all the fakers and smug bastards who think they are better than me! Your mother and I have enough in common boy, but it was our shared pain at being rejected that we bonded over the most! We are a family united by pain, Kevin, not success!"

"Damn it dad, maybe if you were not so damn difficult to be around, then more people would not look down on you, huh? I'm not like you, I'm not so lazy that I'm going to give up trying to be a better person, a *successful* person! I have not figured out the best way to get things to get the ball rolling yet, I'll keep trying till I die as long as I don't end up like… like *you* dad!"

"But no matter how much you bitch and moan about it, you're *my* son and part of this family, Kevin!" Biff roared fanatically. He burst out coughing again and staggered as he got up, but just kept laughing as he had an unhinged look in his eyes. "You're just like me boy, you can fight it all you want but in the end we all end up more like our parents than we want to admit! No matter how much you try and resist Kevin, you're gonna be as bald as me, as fat as me, and at this rate as successful as me because you're as slick as I am! It's just that being hip and popular is not in the Summers genes and your mom's family only did a bit better!

"Why you think all the friends you still hang out with are outcasts themselves, boy? Just come to terms with the fact that you will always be an outsider and find those who will accept you for what you are, Kevin, before you waste the rest of your life chasing fantasies!

"I can't keep you afloat forever. Someday I'll retire one way or another and based on how the markets have been, that means we will have to rely on you providing for the family! So man up and accept what you are! What I want for my birthday more than anything is for you to accept what you are, son!

Accept you're not going to have more than a handful of friends. Accept that you will have to live within your means because you won't make enough money to live in anything bigger than an apartment unless you have the guts to move out west. Accept that you're not going to have a Hollywood love story, but you'll find someone to love, and that's enough at the end of the day. Accept reality already Kevin! Accept reality AND DO THAT DAMN GYM CLASS TO BECOME A REAL MAN!"

Kevin saw that his mother, his uncle, Bart, and Chuck all looked either detached or withdrawn as he gritted his teeth. "How dare you tell me what my life should be, dad! All you do is spit out garbage advice and be a damn hypocrite your entire damn life! Every single thing you said about romance has been wrong, and frankly every idea you had to succeed is wrong since it's not worked so far! What the hell do you even know what it is to be a real man these days? It's not like when you grew up, things have changed and trying to be like how you think things should be will just make the hole I'm in even deeper!

"It's because you don't know a damn thing that things have been so much harder than they had to be in the first place! If I had people that knew what I was doing maybe it would not be so damn difficult! But everyone makes mistakes, what's worse is that you refuse to change!

"You keep doing the same things again and again, you keep thinking the same damn ideas will work when they *never* work! No one outside this table in the entire damn world really respects you, dad! How much more isolated do you have to get before you wake up at last to just how little you have?"

"I don't give a damn what *anyone* thinks about me, boy!" Kevin's dad roared with fury as he turned beet red. "Don't you get it, Kevin? I'm not asking for a lot, but I really don't care what anyone thinks about me, because in the end family's the only people who really stick with you! Family's thicker than blood, Kevin, they are the *only* ones that understand you after everyone else leaves you.

"I don't care how much you're ashamed of me, Kevin. I am who I am, and I'm *still* your father! I'm not going to be what you want me to be, so stop moaning and accept what you are and what your family is! Man up and live the only life you're *going* to have!

"Even if no one else respects me, I'm still your damn father boy! I created you, I own you, and as long as you don't make more money than me you owe it to me, to respect the man of the house no matter how much you don't get my wisdom!"

"I don't care how long it takes, I'll never be like you! I'll…"

"Stop thinking you're better than me, you're my damn son! Stop thinking you can do better than me, you are not going to escape what you are, son! No matter how much you moan about it, you're not what you're not, so accept it! You're no hero or genius, you're just like me. YOU'RE JUST LIKE ME! So, accept what you're going to get in life! You're not going to get that supermodel; you're not going to be famous, Kevin! We are people who are not wanted by most, and if that's the case then screw them, SCREW THEM ALL!"

Kevin saw his dad cough furiously, to the point that it was more of a shrill than a cough. Biff looked delirious, like a man who knew he was powerless and all he could do was scream with pure loathing at everything around him.

Kevin saw with terror that everyone was listening to his father's tirade before a waitress walked up and cleared her throat. "Um, sir should we call a doctor? You don't look well."

Biff just glared at the waitress before he chuckled. "This is how I always look! You're saying I always look like crap? I don't care what you think, I can still eat and I'm not bothering anyone so I'm not going nowhere till I'm done!"

Biff tripped but Bart and Chuck caught him before he fell. Biff hit the table so hard some of the meatballs got stuck to his face and some of the tomato sauce splashed on his right shoulder. Kevin winced. "Damn it dad, let's just finish talking when we are not around people that can hear you."

Biff looked around, and only looked angrier by the second.

"You think you're so much better than me when you're only able to live because of me, boy? I don't care if you're ashamed of me, Kevin, I'm not hurting anybody so I'm going to stay till dinner is over!"

"Please, we will just talk about it later in the week, right mom?"

His mother was just slowly drinking before she answered. "You can, but I won't be here. I told you I'm going to visit Uncle Evan for a week?"

"Wait, what? You're just leaving for a week? But it's a horrible week to…"

"I *need* a change of pace, Kevin. You know full well how taxing things can be at home and my brother was nice enough to get a deal for me, so I took it. Maybe you two can work it out while I'm gone."

"There's nothing to talk about," Biff slurred out. 'Just be a man, Kevin, give up your kid dreams already and be a real man. Stop being a boy and be a real man who respects his father. Even if no one else in the damn world respects me you must respect your father, YOU HAVE TO! That's the only thing that matters, it's the *only* thing!"

"Mom please, don't leave when he's this messed up."

"Kevin, you know he doesn't listen to me. One way or another something's got to give, so I'll leave and see who's backed down by the time I'm back."

"Damn it, I'm always stuck picking things up with no real answer on how to break through. You know how stressful it's been on me?"

"The world does not care, man," Bart threw out carefully as he casually drank more beer. "The cold truth is no one cares about moaning, either deal or fold."

Kevin saw how indifferent his friend looked as the stress built up in his head and he held it in pain. Then he started coughing as he grasped his chest. "Well for now, I'll deal by going to the bathroom because you're all stressing me the hell out. Thank god your little meltdown was not in front of too many people! Damn it, like I don't have enough to deal with. Do you know how much you stress me out dad? One day you keep pushing it and you're going to give me a stroke or something."

"Trust someone who legit had a heart attack, Kevin, the stress you feel now is not going to give you one. Besides, better for me if you're too stressed out to try and screw me over when I'm older! If you're a good son, you will repay the debts you owe your father till he dies! If you can't pay enough for a good old folk's home, boy, *you're* going to be the one to look after us!"

"Damn it, and waste away my life till I'm a husk? What happens if I'm so spent my life's nearly over when yours is?"

"Not my problem boy."

Kevin was about to explode before he saw people were still looking at him. He used all of his willpower to keep quiet. With a glare at his father, Kevin walked off to the bathroom, but little did he realize as bad as things were, they were about to get much worse.

While he was going to the bathroom, Chandler walked by and went back to where he was eating with Alison in a section that Chandler paid to keep private.

Alison was completely oblivious to Kevin's current situation, and just raised an eyebrow as he walked back. "What took you so long? Did you get a phone call? I heard shouting, was there a fight?"

"Relax love, there was a fight, but it's something to laugh about rather than fret about. Some local bumpkin was arguing with his son in a rather loud manner. It was so pathetic that it was hilarious really, so hilarious that I had to record it on my phone! This local is so pathetic, I think I can work it into my blog, Ali!"

Alison raised an eyebrow before Chandler showed her the footage he recorded, before she gasped at horror. Despite the fact that the man in front of her was fatter and balder than she remembered, she quickly realized who was yelling before she cringed. "Oh god, he's here?"

"You know this loser, babe? What! Not some stalker causing you grief on the set? Just say the word and he will rue that for the rest of his pathetic life."

"No wait calm down, Chandler. I don't quite know him, he's just the father of a friend of mine."

"Oh, the bloke that this lard was ranting at? So you *were* friends with him? Guess this town really does not have much to offer, huh?"

"Hey, don't be like that. Kevin was, is my friend. He doesn't have your charm, but he always was there for me and tried his best to make me happy."

"Is that so Alison?" Chandler said coolly. "Well, it's nice you had someone looking out for you before our fates crossed and all, but trying is one thing, but doing is another. That Yoda bloke was on to something after all, there is no try, only do, or something.

"From this not so small chat it seems your childhood chump, or chum, has done a lot of trying without a lot of doing. If he *really* wanted it, he would have not been looking like a fool. When my papa lectured me, *I* listened."

Alison took a deep breath as she remembered all she saw of Kevin since she came back. "Oh, come on Chandler…don't be that way. Not everyone starts in the same place in life and all."

"True, my father's success gave me a few more advantages than others, Ali, but you came from far less stellar circumstances and still blossomed to the stellar rose you are now, while this dullard failed to even leave the nest. Some are strong enough to grasp their dreams, and others are too weak to do anything but try and mask their failures.

"Of course, when those who pretend to be what they are not prance around the real thing, they end up looking like quite the pathetic posers. Ah, yes he's the same chap who Carlos said came to the get together you all had a few days ago and all but *begged* for a job?

"He really wants things, I see, but sadly he's about to learn effort is not enough when you don't have the style to be worth it. Today showed he clearly comes from a family without any style at all."

Alison thought of how excited Kevin looked when he was talking with Carlos and the others before she got defensive. "Chandler, you're getting the wrong idea. I'd appreciate it if you don't talk about my friend as if he is a pathetic bum. I invited him to the party and he, well, he's not you, but he did not drag the party down or anything.

"True he's down on his luck and he might not have the raw charisma to pull off something on your level, but it's not like he's not trying hard, it's not like he's worthless! He's good at history, writing, acting, and…"

"And everything else that's not really important these days, right dear? Sorry, no need to be rude but as sad as it is, aside from the cream of the crop, all other artists are more like a side job for winners these days. Liberal arts degrees might as well be called degrees for second class citizens because the cold truth is that's what they are compared to the winners of the world."

"Well, we *all* grew up still under the impression that the world valued more than a few kinds of jobs okay? Please, I want to help him."

"You really are a sweetheart. Well, good thing you're not the boss, sometimes the boss has to turn their heart off to get business done, including showing people just what they deserve. But if this Kevin wants his fifteen minutes of fame so badly, I can surely help with that. Like I said, this rant could fit well into my blog, and by the end of it will be a nice little segment on TMX as a short on local fools making a fool of themselves."

"What? Please, don't put something on your blog to make Kevin and his family look bad. I don't want Kevin; I just don't want the people in this town to think I came back here just to mock them."

"Smart, thinking of your image love. No worries, I'm not about to put *you* in a bad position. But we can't let people keep running around in their dream worlds, ok? Spotlights helps gals like you get seen for what you are, and this other venture just helps those like Kevin be seen for what they really are. Not quite as glamorous an outcome for sure, but, it's all someone like him can get and it's best he understands that sooner than later. After all it's not like you can let this Kevin guy keep assuming things, right?"

"Of course not. I just want him to see how things are in the least painful way possible."

Chandler replayed the video to see Kevin from behind arguing with his father, and as he saw Kevin's dad yell deliriously his eyes narrowed. "But of course, love. Alas, sometimes the truth hurts, and people only learn when they learn loud and clear where they belong. Don't worry, by the end it will be clear for everyone. But that's *not* part of tonight, so let's just have a good time, okay, Ali?"

Alison saw Chandler grin and could not help but feel entranced by his smile before she put her thoughts of Kevin out of her head. "Right Chandler. Can't make everyone happy, so just got to focus on what you can do."

"Now you're sounding like a winner, Ali. Can't get ahead if you try and stop for every sap who's not as lucky as you. And if they protest, then you just gotta shove reality in their face till they can't hide any longer. One way or another, it will be a fun way to cap things out here, right? As they say, got to milk things for what they're worth. And when it's done, everything will be clear, for *everyone*."

9

Stepping into Reality's Harsh Spotlight

Kevin was so demoralized by his father's outburst that after a quick round of responding to emails he fell asleep, or at least tried to amidst all the frustration he was feeling. It was his hopes for things to work out with Alison that gave him enough peace to fall asleep.

Despite being tired, Kevin got up early, so he did not have to look at his father and start off the day on a sour note. When he got to work he looked for Alison. He was dismayed as he saw that many people seemed to be whispering and snickering upon seeing him.

Kevin didn't even look them in the eye and tried to keep calm by assuring himself that they could be laughing at something else. However, seeing people point at their phone while looking in his direction did not help Kevin keep the tide of anxiety at bay.

Kevin's mood lifted as he saw Alison talking with Cammy. But just before he could attempt to see her, he saw a guy walk up to her from her right.

Seeing how quickly Alison smiled at him caused Kevin to freeze in his tracks. A painful reminder of just how slim his chances for Alison to return his feelings crept across his mind. He was trying to decide if it was worth trying to talk to Alison, but his choice was made for him as he saw Bright walking over to him. "Here I thought I snoozed off, Kevin, but seems you are early for once! Guess I owe Sam that dollar."

"Hey Bright," Kevin said as he straightened up. "Morning. I guess I just wanted to give a good impression and start things off on the right foot and all."

Bright saw that some people behind Kevin were pointing at him and snickering after looking at their phones. "Kid, we don't always get to leave the impression we want to make. Sometimes, people have an impression of us before we even meet them, and nothing we do will change it. But as long as your job's not public relations stuff, then your job comes first and center. Kevin, everything else is just extra credit, and that don't mean jack if you don't get done what matters. You get what I'm trying to say?"

"Yeah, of course Bright," Kevin answered with an uneasy chuckle. "The job comes before anything else. Can't argue with results, right? So, I'll start by asking Carlos what he wants and take it from there."

"Sounds good to me, kid. Just contact me if anything goes haywire, ok?"

"Got it."

Kevin moved past his boss and looked around for Carlos. Sam went up to Bright and asked, "Do you think the kid knows?"

"Don't know, but unless he asks, I'm not about to be the one that ruins his day. Talk about making a mess of things."

"Ah come on Bright, not his fault some punk took a video of him without him knowing. Hell, some wiseass tried to do the same thing when my ma thought she was at school. Only reason he stopped is because even a wiseass punk can change his mind about a photo when you make it clear what you're going to do to someone taking advantage of your mom acting out cause of dementia. Hell, if I knew which smartass uploaded the video, I might have a word with him."

"I would too Sam, but the fact is we don't," Bright said bluntly. "So other than reminding these Starlight fellas to be professional, we just got to make sure Kevin can keep it under control no matter what happens."

"Well, so far these guys and gals seem to be on the level."

"Yah, the ones we've seen so far," Bright said as he saw Chandler laugh brazenly in the distance. "But when they keep having extra crew joining up without telling us the game's changed, could at least give us a heads up, but guess the big shots rarely give a damn what the help thinks, huh? Whatever, long as they don't slow down production, I don't give a damn. Alright, where's that damn grip? Are we going to shoot or just *talk* about shooting all day?"

Chandler grumbled before looking for his crew. As he did, Kevin managed to find Carlos a minute later. The finale to the Starlight photo shoot took place in a local closed down supermarket that had been abandoned for years and was being remodeled for the photo shoot to show the future of fashion, if not society.

Kevin found Carlos in what used to be the manager's office and saw him talking to a few women before he cleared his throat. "Hey Carlos, sorry if it's a bad time."

Carlos saw Kevin looked uneasy and just laughed. "How can it be a bad time when we are all about to have a blast, man? C'mon man, if I asked for you here, why would I think it's a bad time for you to show up?"

Kevin saw Carlos was sincere and loosened up. "Fair point. Same game plan as before then?"

"You got it, amigo. Aside from Cammy, the order's the same. Just check with us to make sure the angle's right and it's clear, got it."

Kevin looked out the window before he said. "Got it. Man! *Never* thought this place would be crowded again. Figured they would have torn this place down by now. Well, good thing it's taken so long for people to figure out what to do, huh?"

"This place may have been nothing but a relic of the old era for a while now, Kevin, but Starlight's turning it into a beacon of the future, man! Well, for a moment at least but hey, better to have a moment in the spotlight than none, right?"

Kevin's smile eroded a bit, then he just chuckled bitterly. "Well, depends on how everyone looks at you when you're in the light, right? Well, better make sure everyone looks good in the light today, right? I'll text you if anything comes up."

Carlos gave Kevin a thumbs up before dashing out. Another member of Starlight was about to say something before a voice cut in with a sharp "Man, the bloke's as eager as a puppy to please."

Carlos saw Chandler walk in from the other office before shrugging. "Sure, you can see the tension in his face, man, but hell, not like we get that kind of reaction *every* time we come to a town that has not seen a lot of action in a while, huh?"

"True…but most are not delusional enough to think they can just join us."

"Hey, no need to go loco about it, Chandler. Getting a job's all about being persistent, right?"

"True, but it's also about knowing what you can do and what you can't. When you're being a fool, you're a true fool to not think you will be treated like one. Guess the world is seeing him for what he is?"

"I mean, that's because *you* took a video of him and his pa, right amigo?"

"I mean his father was causing such a scene, a lot of people saw it."

"Yeah, but Alison told me you uploaded the video right to your "Clown of the Week" site for making fools out of people?"

"Oh, Ali told you that? Well, it's for the best, really. Any random chump may have uploaded a video, but at least it will be uploaded with style!"

"Man, you *really* think he will see it that way if he finds out?"

"That's what the fans will think and that's *all* that matters."

"C'mon man, he's been helpful so far. Screwing him over seems kind of poor taste, you know?"

"You always did go the extra mile for everyone, Carlos. It's why you're the best at our marketing. Still, *I'm* the best one at making every event as profitable as can be, right? There's *nothing* profitable about letting pretenders clown around. If he makes a fuss he will be crushed. Enough about him, we got a climax to kick off! Should be a show, all right."

"Yeah…just hope it's the right kind of show."

"It is for Alison and the rest of the gals and their fans; does it *really* matter what is right for throwaway bit players?"

With a shrug, Carlos helped Chandler go through final preparations, and the final Starlight show in Springfield kicked off.

***

As the high-ranking members of Starlight went through their final preparations, another member was going through the same thing, albeit a different kind of preparation.

Alison was with Cammy and the others doing final preparations on their outfits.

Cammy saw Alison hastily zip up the back of her outfit, before she saw another co-worker nearly trip and rolled her eyes. "Oh, c'mon Alison, don't let your pose slip now. Keeping one's composure here, let me help you before you rip something."

Cammy got behind her, and Alison gave a sheepish grin. "Sorry Cammy, just the nerves, you know?"

"Here I thought you were taking on the mindset of a pro, but your nerves are fraying if this is getting to you. We performed for big people in big cities. A small joint like this should be nothing for you by now."

Alison thought about her time so far back in her old hometown before she let out a sigh of melancholy. "I know it should feel like that, Cammy, but it's just that I'm wondering if I pulled this tour off enough to make the progress I was hoping for. And if not, how many is it going to take?"

"You're wondering how many times you have to prance around in the middle of nowhere before you can call the shots? I can relate, I have had more than my fill with hicks. Still, you have great relations with many of the powers that be Alison, I'm sure that will help you move things along."

"C'mon Cammy, Chandler's not someone I see just as a tool. Besides, it's more than having enough people pushing me to a higher position, will this help get enough fans and get me closer to being a star."

"Ah, well that's the million-dollar question right, girl? Well, it's all about getting enough people to like you till important people like you. Got to keep being active and relevant till it pays off. If that means impressing a dead-end town with a flashy send off to make them think they are more than nobodies, then that's just another part of the job."

"I, guess you're right. Only thing to do is to do the job right."

"Good, so adjust your mask and let's get this show on the road already."

Alison saw Cammy adjust her own dress before walking out, then she looked at herself in the mirror and reflected on Cammy's advice.

What Cammy says makes sense, it's how Jessica went on to star in Pitch Perfect Five after all. She seems happy on her Instagram. If Chandler can deliver, this time next year I might be in a movie myself.

And then Kevin and guys like him can say they knew a superstar growing up. Kevin, I know he always liked movies. Is this what he thought being in showbiz would be like? I guess in the end that does not really matter much.

Despite her thoughts, Alison could not help but feel conflicted. But before she could lament more, her co-workers called for her and she got ready for the show.

***

Kevin only heard hints from Alison and the others about what the final shoot would be about. But he and all the other locals saw that it was without a doubt worth the wait. Alison's co-worker strutted out in an elegant green dress with extensions that nearly had her come off as a humanoid peacock.

Cammy had enough skin to get eyes drawn to what was exposed, while still having enough concealed to cause her audience to wonder.

As she went to the front of the platform and did a few playful poses, the speakers boomed, "Our dear Cammy is rising like a phoenix! Each of today's Starlight ladies are dressed up in very special outfits that are all based from deities from all kinds of cultures. It's a way to show our stars are both inspired by the legends of the past, while seeking to be trailblazers of the future!"

As Cammy did a few more poses, Kevin saw other models strut in following Cammy, all in various neon colored outfits with faint ties to animals. Kevin knew most of their names after covering the past few shoots but was diligent in making sure he covered them all properly on camera.

While he had been steeling himself to not lose focus the entire time, as the lights dimmed, he could not help but look in awe as Alison at last walked onto the stage. Her special outfit was a striking magenta and black dress with a small swan-like mask. Kevin had to use all his will power to not clap or cheer as he saw her gracefully strut forward.

As she walked up and did a playful dance move, the announcer boomed an excited, "And for the Coupe de grace of our show we have our very lovely Alison Winters! The Black Swan is infamously known as a creature of tragedy in many stories. But Alison here, as the regal swan of the future, is going to soar to untold heights. She's symbolizing how all ducklings can rise up from their humble origins to become fabulous superstars!"

Kevin observed Alison intently. As she waltzed past him, he tried to play it cool as he saw the backside of her outfit.

Man…I knew they would save the best for last, but this is legit out of this world. After seeing so many crazy outfits in movies, I always figured they could hardly move in most of them. But guess that's just for someone clumsy like me, Alison's graceful enough to pull off anything.

Kevin's train of thought was cut off as he noticed Alison was staggering just a little on her way back. He then saw that one of the previous models made a small hole in the ground from her claw-shaped boot. Alison now seemed briefly distracted in her effort to keep her poise and did not seem to realize she was about to walk into the hole.

With no time to call out, Kevin on instinct dashed forward just as she tripped. Alison fell right off the stage, but Kevin managed to catch her. He fell in the process, but he managed to land without either of them sustaining any injuries.

Alison had fallen so fast she could just barely comprehend what had happened. But as she saw Kevin had her by the shoulders she coughed, "K—Kevin?"

"Alison…are you alright?"

"Yeah, though that might change after I see how the dress looks."

"Oh…sorry about that."

Alison saw how worried Kevin looked before she smiled. "Why are you sorry? Unless you're the one who tripped me, seems like you got me out of a real jam. Thanks Kevin, I admit I did not think you could pull off the dramatic save stuff."

"I'm no football player but I have tried to work out enough to not be useless. Just didn't want to see you hurt."

"Thanks…but my image's going to be hurt after that mess up."

"I mean, it's not live, right? We can just edit it out and all. C'mon Alison, not like I would have your big moment make you look bad."

Alison looked touched at that, and Kevin saw she looked sincerely happy. But before she could respond a sharp voice shouted, "Get off her!"

Kevin saw Cammy, Chandler, and many others running up to the two. Half of them had worried expressions, while the rest sprouted angry enough looks to cause Kevin to flinch. As Kevin hastily got back on his feet, Chandler's previous swagger-filled smile was nearly completely overwritten with a scowl of raw contempt. "Think you're rather slick, mate?" Cammy just rolled her eyes as she crossed her arms. "Really now, you're so desperate you had to pull a stunt like this?"

Alison saw how Kevin was already turning pale before she cleared her throat. "C'mon guys, lay off Kevin. He just helped make this not be as bad as it could have been. I tripped 'cause my shoe got stuck on the floor! I told you the slippers were too tight!"

Chandler looked baffled for a few moments. The idea that Alison would defend Kevin didn't even cross his mind. But he regained his poise and crossed his arms. "Oh, I see now. Having second thoughts, Ali? I thought after how much we worked on the outfit you would have every detail memorized."

"C'mon Chandler, it was more your idea than mine. I mean, you wanted the animal to be like your family logo."

"I thought it was something we both worked on together to highlight *both* of our talents?"

"Well…that is true. I guess it's just things sometimes things look differently after seeing them from different angles. Look, the dress is fine so just fix the damn floor and let's make up for lost time already."

Cammy saw Alison flick her hair back before she said. "You never did like to have anything keep you down, right, girl? That's the sprit. C'mon on, make sure that floor is safe, damn it!"

Alison and Chandler got talking about the dress. Kevin saw that she didn't seem to remember he was still there. He realized people were still looking at him before he gave a sheepish grin and went back to the camera. Aside from a few wisecracks from Sam, no one gave him too much hassle for the mishap and the recording quickly resumed.

When it resumed, Chandler guided Alison behind the camera, and while Kevin thought he saw Alison's eye twitch, she pulled off her second attempt flawlessly.

Even though Kevin saw her walk just minutes before, he and most of the people around her had to exert most of their willpower to keep on task. After Alison finished her run, she returned to the stage with Cammy and the rest of the Starlight models.

The ladies all got into position to do a group pose as the announcer eagerly said, "And so with this outburst of beauty we mark the end of Starlight's time in Springfield! While our time in this town will end, we hope our touches will inspire everyone enough to let their own style erupt! Have fun figuring it out!"

After some of the lights went off, some of the ladies cheered at completing another shoot. Kevin saw Alison looked tired. He made sure his camera was off and thought, *Damn…its over already.*

Before Kevin could stew any longer in his thoughts, he saw Carlos come in with a wide grin. "That's a wrap, gals! Way to end in style!

126

Well, had a few bumps in the road but hey, life's not flawless right? And it's because of that imperfection that people appreciate true beauty even more, right? So stumbles are part of true grace and all that."

Alison saw a few of her coworkers giggling before she flicked some hair out of her eye. "Sorry for that Carlos, I think the mask clouded my vision a little."

"Hey, no worries, not like it was live or anything. Long as nothing's broken, just another learning experience. Still, guess it's because of Kevin that it just ended with that. Guess you were at the right place at the right time, huh amigo?"

Kevin saw Carlos was being sincere and he smiled with relief. "I'm glad luck threw me a bone at the right time, man. I'm just glad you guys were able to let me take part in legit quality work. It was a blast."

"Glad you're grateful, Kevin, but why are you saying your goodbyes already, dude? Show's over, but Starlight's got one last fling going on. I mean, we're having the wrap up party tonight, for everyone who worked on the project."

"S-seriously?"

"What's with the shocked look, man? Does Starlight seem like tacaños to you?"

Chandler saw Kevin's shock before he flashed a polished grin. "True we can afford a big party Carlos, but don't you think it's fair that only people that are part of our family take part? After all it would be cruel to give people a taste of what can't last."

"C'mon man, for now they are one of us, and maybe it will help inspire them to push harder. Alright, you down for showing up at six at the Vault at the Springfield Hotel?"

"Of course! Hard to forget when there only a few places like that around. Glad I can have another blast before you guys leave."

Alison's saw Kevin's excitement before she hesitated. "Well, it's not going to be quite the same as at the one at Sweet Track, Kevin. Since it's a wrap up party it might be a bit more intense."

"That so Alison? Well, might not be my usual style, but I'll try and hang on if I can. After all, don't have much lined up after this, so want to enjoy every moment of this while it lasts."

Alison smiled, but she saw a sorrowful look on Kevin's face. "Ah don't be sad Kevin; you're acting like this is the last day of your life or something."

Kevin winced as he chuckled and looked down. "Well I would hope I'm not dying tomorrow, Alison. I'm sure my life won't end anytime soon, but I have to act like it is at times to live life to the fullest, right?"

"Ha, that's a winning mindset, dude! Just make sure you can see it through."

"Thanks Carlos, I'll go get ready right now."

Alison giggled as she leaned forward. "Don't be too eager, Kevin. I mean, things are mostly wrapped up on our end but what about your side?"

Kevin winced as he looked back at the camera. "Oh right, better clear things with Bright first."

Alison saw Kevin go for the camera, only for his hand to twitch and lose its grip. She saw Kevin's arm twitch before she raised an eyebrow. "Are, are you okay, Kevin? You—you did not get injured catching me, did you?"

"What this?" Kevin threw out coyly. "Nah, don't worry about it. It's nothing major. Just I've had a back problem for a few years. Nothing major, just, my spine feels shifted at times, so it can affect my arms and legs a bit."

"What, seriously? What has the doctor said about it?"

"I don't know. It happened after I fell off my parents' health insurance. I can't really afford any advance stuff at the moment. I mean, I have checked a few back doctors. I'm not sure they are that great though, might have made it worse. It's just another reminder to keep pushing till I break through. Just a little while longer, almost there."

Kevin had a driven look as he grasped his hand and went to contact Bright. Alison saw him walk out of the room, she winced as some of her coworkers giggled behind Kevin's back.

Kevin…he's really pushing himself so hard he's about to break? Damn it, I want to be able to help him, I just don't know how. I can't make his dreams come true, but I don't want to leave him broken either. I hope I can find a middle ground; he deserves that much at least.

Alison ceased her musing as she saw Chandler strutting over. As she figured out the best way to proceed with Chandler, Kevin was trying to do the same. He swiftly returned his gear to the company van and made sure everything was in its proper place, he reflected on how the final shoot went out.

While Chandler and some of the others gave him some rather intense looks, the fact that Alison seemed happy overrode everything else he went through and he grasped his hand confidently.

Alison seemed impressed with how things turned out. Some of the new guys seemed rather dismissive, but Carlos seems cool. If I can seal the deal tonight, I might just be able to make it. Maybe Carlos can help me get a real job. And if I can pull that off, just maybe I'll have a chance with Alison. I know if all the other girls dismissed me then as things are now Alison won't likely want to date me, but if I can just prove I can be a somebody.

Kevin heard two men snickering. He saw the taller man that seemed to be one of the newer Starlight members snickering as he pointed out something to the shorter man. Kevin raised an eyebrow as he made sure nothing on him looked out of order before he cleared his throat. "Hey guys, is there a problem or something?"

"Nah dude, just laughing at a funny ass joke."

"Sorry, my face look like a punchline or something?" Kevin retorted with restraint as he slowly walked up to the two. The taller one saw the anger in Kevin's eyes before he spat on the ground. "Nah, but it looks like it's part of a joke on here, dude!"

The man flipped his phone around, and Kevin was mortified to see himself. It was an image of him arguing with his father. He saw his dad's tantrum up to where the meatballs were stuck to his head flash back from a different angle, and saw that the video title was, Local loser family squabble, Kevin grit his teeth. "You…you posted this online?"

The two men saw the fury amassing in Kevin's eyes and their mocking moods quickly shifted as a result. As Kevin moved closer, the taller man gulped. "Hey, chill dude, don't shoot the messenger, okay? We just saw the video on the ten jokers of the day, man! Sorry dude, you were in the wrong place at the wrong time. Hey, if you act fast maybe you can get a chunk of the ad revenue, right?"

Kevin watched the rest of the video before he grasped his fist tightly. "Something tells me that's not going to happen at this point. Damn it!"

Kevin quickly took out his own phone and looked up the video. He saw the video had a lot of likes, but that the comments were flooded with people mocking Kevin and his father as clowns.

Kevin saw people were around and quickly went into his car. He gave a low moan as he slouched into his seat.

No, damn it, why now of all times? This is not how I wanted to make a name for myself. If Alison has not seen this yet, no way someone would not have shown her by tonight. I mean, I'm not really doing anything wrong, but it just makes me look like a total joke. Damn it, dad, you always, always ruin everything.

But because of this, I might be screwed not just out of this job, but a lot of other jobs. Now I must be even more careful. If I do this wrong then not only will Alison reject me, it might be even harder to get out of the pit my life's been in ever since I got out of college.

No, it can't be too late, I can't let my chance at having a better life slip away. I, won't end up like my uncle, otherwise what life is there to look forward to? Just got to figure out a way to get out of this. There has to be, a way.

Kevin grasped the car wheel so tightly his fingernails left marks on the rubber as he frantically tried to figure out how to not have everything he had been working for go up in flames.

10

One's Place in the World

Once he cleared everything with Bright, Kevin got home as soon as he could. He told his parents he needed to take a nap but could hardly keep his eyes closed with how frustrated he was. Everything he worked for was at risk because of something that was out of his control. After lamenting long enough, he was able to get his emotions under control. Kevin went to get ready and try to do everything he could to have his dreams come true.

After showering, Kevin managed to get Bart to tag along, mostly after assuring him the food and most of the drinks were free. As Kevin finished getting dressed in his nicest jeans and dress shirt, he saw Bart had not changed. He raised an eyebrow. "Hey Bart, you going to change soon?"

"I *already* changed, bro."

"But you have not done anything yet."

"C'mon pay attention dude! I gelled my hair! What, this some ballroom dance?"

"Well no, but still, Bart, it *is* supposed to be one where everyone's supposed to dress to impress and all."

"What, I'm not the one conning myself thinking a supermodel's going to fall for me, man. I'm going as who I am, if people don't like that then it's their loss."

"C'mon man, was hoping you could be my wing-man and help me."

"I'm not going to do anything to ruin your chances, man, but not going the extra mile either. I mean c'mon man, do I look like I'm a part of those people to you?"

"Well, I guess you do look like you're going to another party. Guess this is not really your thing."

"Sure as hell not. To be perfectly honest I'm not willing to back something that's got no chance of happening anyway."

"C'mon Bart, can't you at least *try* and act like I have a shot of pulling it off?"

"What can I say, man? I used to pretend to give a crap, but after those two or four other girls all vanished on you year after year when you were sure things were going somewhere might as well be honest about it."

"Bart. . . you know you really suck at this whole friend thing at times."

"Just being honest at how much you sucked at this so far, Kevin. Want me to brag about your nonexistent success so far? What, you got anyone else lined up that can help you pull this off? In the end you asked me because you don't really have *any* backup wingman standing by, huh?"

"Well...maybe Guile would be a better fit, but I think he said he had something going on with his family."

"So yeah, I'm *all* you got, dude. Relax, I'll be chilling with the less uptight guys in the crew. At the very least I can drive you back if you get wasted."

"Thanks, but I don't think I'll start drinking tonight, man. With how fragile things are, have to be as in control as I can if I hope to salvage this."

"Being uptight is not going to help, bro. Might as well just take it for what it is instead of a hopeless dream, right?"

Kevin saw Bart had a casual smirk and all the tension he felt since Alison came back surged across his face. Kevin could barely contain his frustration as he shouted, "Damn it, Bart, this is *not* a joke! This is the best chance, and what might be the *last* chance I have to turn my life around! Can't you at least not take it as a joke and try and help a little!?"

To Kevin's dismay, Bart just chuckled in response. "Hey man, I can tell you're serious about it, but don't think you can get people to think things you think are important are as important to them. Don't think this is like a movie where I can pull a trick out of my ass to get everything to smell like roses.

"Look man…I get you want things to work out badly, but if you want it too badly then everyone will see how desperate you are and it's all downhill from there. Just be realistic and all, dude, and take whatever comes like a man."

Kevin looked despondent for a moment before he nodded. "I…I get what you mean, Bart. Guess losing my cool won't help anything, right? Shouting like an idiot won't help nudge Alison to like me or help persuade Carlos to want to hire me, so at least if I play it cool it might look good down the line, right?"

"Glad you're able to be on the level, man. At least no matter how it goes you won't lose your pride, am I right? Don't worry about me, don't want to make too big an impression either way since I'm going to be going to the next phase of my life. Soon, I'll be where I should be."

"Oh, really Bart? What makes you think this time it will work better than in Texas or Florida?"

"Have a little faith, bro!"

Kevin winced as he said. "No offense Bart, but if it's fair to say I keep going in circles how come I have to keep expecting things to go as you say?"

Bart snickered before he patted Kevin on the back so hard it nearly knocked him over. "Really dude? It's 'cause I'm not a follower like you Kevin, I'm a man of action!"

Kevin grit his teeth, but before he could retort, his father made a loud burp. Biff saw his son's sudden look and sneered. "I told you from the start to not get your hopes up, boy! Damn it, you're so worked up you're being careless. You let the cable go out again because you put your crap on the cable box again and blocked the transmission right when the show was getting good!"

Kevin saw that his dad was pointing at the cable box, and that Kevin's laptop was next to it. Kevin rolled his eyes. "First of all, dad, my stuff is *not* crap! And damn it all, nothing is blocking your damn cable!"

"You're disrespecting me lying to my face, boy? I see your stuff right next to the box!"

"That doesn't matter dad! I told you, it's not on the cable, it's not blocking anything! The waves don't work that way, damn it! Stop being so damn…"

"ENOUGH WITH THE DISRESPECT, BOY!" His dad roared as his eye twitched. "The cable's not working cause *you're* blocking the waves! You think I'm stupid!? I'm so goddamn sick of you mocking me! You have no goddamn reason to be acting like this!"

"Really? Because of how you acted you made us both look like a joke!"

"I don't care how I act, if people don't like it it's their problem!"

"And it's my problem because I look like a joke because of *you*!"

"Not my fault you aim for people you don't belong with! You should care more about the man who brought you into this world! But you're always looking at me with those ungrateful eyes! You should look at me with the same respect Bucky had when I got home!"

"Dad, when you say Bucky, are you talking about your childhood dog? I'm not a god damn dog!"

"I know, you should have even more respect for me then Bucky cause I made you! You should be looking at me with goddamn gratitude for giving you life! Respect me, damn it, respect your damn father!"

"Damn it dad, I'm not going to spend my life shackled to you! That's why I'm doing all this, so I can be with people I like being with like..."

"Like Alison? Bah, Alison was *never* the right girl for you, and you just keep going for her cause of her pretty face! Hell, now you want to work for some prissy models? You never talked about any of that crap before Alison showed up out of the blue again. You're not thinking with your head, boy!"

"I'm thinking I have to try *something* dad!" Kevin blasted at his father. "You're the one who told me again and again I can't be too picky, so that's why I'm willing to stomach a few things that are not ideal to get things to take off!"

"Damn it boy, I did not mean just throw darts at everything you saw and hope *something* sticks! You're not part of their world Kevin, just accept which world you're a part of already and find how to live in *that* one!"

Memories of seeing the online video of his father caused Kevin to turn beet red as he seethed. "Maybe if you bothered to not make things so goddamn difficult, my world would not be so far apart from them, dad! Maybe if you did just a little more than belch out things to make you feel good, maybe the hole I'm in would not be so damn deep!"

"It would go better if you just did not moan about every damn thing and respected me already! RESPECT YOUR FATHER!"

"If you're not going to change dad, then why would I magically change to respect the person that's *never* going to change?"

"Because even *my* patience will run out if you don't realize how grateful you should be to me!"

Biff made a dramatic hand gesture, which knocked over a vase Kevin got from his last trip. As it broke, Kevin's jaw dropped before he turned red. "Dad, that was the vase I got from the end of the trip to Greece!"

As Kevin turned red, his father had veins form on his forehead. "Don't give me that look, DON'T LOOK AT ME LIKE THAT! It was a piece of crap anyway, despite what you kept saying the girl *never* got back to you!"

"Dad...that was the best time I had last year, and you broke it like it was nothing."

"It's just overpriced bait for tourists that you got suckered into. The memories would be enough if you were not so damn insecure. A real man does not need to have junk all over his place, knowing he did his part should be all he needs, ALL HE NEEDS! If you don't start changing your tune, Kevin, and stop moaning for all the things you will never have and be grateful for what you do have I might get fed up and take *everything* away till you wake up!"

Kevin's father was ranting so intensely, spit was spewing all over the floor. Kevin's eye twitched as he walked up to his dad, before his mother got in front of her husband with an exasperated look. "Stop beating a dead horse, Kevin. Look, he can get carried away at times, but he is right about the biggest things. In the end, your dad is not the kind of guy who knows people, and soon I'm going to be retired so you just don't have any family connections to help. This is just where we are."

"It doesn't have to be mom! Not if we just push a little harder too."

"I'm *tired* of pushing Kevin," his mother responded. "I'm a woman in her sixties, I know who I am. Maybe there could be more to life if I pushed harder, but I'm just too tired. I can't change everything, but I can change how much dust I see, that's all I really care about now, because cleanliness is next to godliness.

I may not be rich but at least, at least I'll be clean. Call me weak, I don't care anymore I just want my days to have as little stress as they can in this world. That includes you, son. I'm too tired to see you waste time on dead ends that make things stressful over nothing. So, you either make this work out or accept being a librarian already."

"Mom, we went over this. No matter what, a librarian is not what I want my life to be about. The life Aunt…"

"My sister might not have made being a clerk seem like a thrilling life, Kevin, but it was her choices that brought her the life she had, not her job. A job like a clerk is just the kind of job that fits our family."

"You mean a life in the shadows? That's not my life, I'll prove it's not my life, if I can just get the chance!"

Bart chuckled as he glanced at the TV past Kevin. "Well, the blunt truth is that your life's been nothing but empty talk, Kevin, why the hell should anyone have any faith in you?"

Kevin glanced at Bart with exasperation as he cracked his neck. "C'mon man, you're supposed to be on my side at least a bit of the time!"

"Since your dad gives the drinks, that means I'm on his side when it counts, dude! What, you don't really have control over anything when it comes down to it, huh, bro? Don't get me wrong, it can be fun chilling out, but just be honest and admit on your own you can't really do jack at the moment."

"Damn it, I can, if things just worked out for once in my goddamn life!"

"Well, at this rate all you're going to prove is that you spent all day ranting about doing things instead of doing them."

"Damn, it's getting late and I *can't* be late for this. Look, after this, I'll have *nothing* but time to talk about things, so see you guys later."

Kevin made sure everything was in order before he and Bart drove to the last party the Starlighters were hosting. Bart threw off a few jokes to pass the time, but Kevin only gave shallow responses as he tried to keep his worries at bay.

Before he knew it, he was at the Vault. While he had been to the local bar/hotel a few times over the years for everything from Boy Scout dinners to funerals, from the moment he parked, he saw this would be a different experience as the building had Starlight logos outside.

Bart saw some stylishly dressed ladies enter the building before he whistled. "Damn man, thought the filming was over?"

Kevin saw one of Alison's co-workers talking to someone outside before he smirked. "It is, but I guess the staff's talking to people about the production. I mean, Starlight's a big deal, so only natural they would get reporters and bloggers from all over. That's what it means to be in the big leagues and all. Time to try and join them."

Kevin walked to the entrance before two large guys stopped them. Since one had a list, Kevin only assumed they were acting as the bouncers, and could not help but tense up as the taller man looked down on him. "Sorry, but if you're not invited to this party, I'm gonna have to ask you to leave."

Kevin chuckled tensely as he tugged his collar. "Sorry for the misunderstanding but I should be on the list. I'm Kevin Summers."

"I don't see that name under Starlight employees."

"That's true, but I've been working with Starlight, I'm from the local TV station."

"C'mon dude, you can't just say you worked with them because you saw one of their gigs."

His co-worker eyed Kevin before he chuckled. "Hold it Raul, I saw a video of that guy! That's right they did say someone they were working with was in a video!"

The man named Raul snorted before he looked at more of the list. He saw Kevin starting to look uneasy before he snickered out, "Damn, *you're* the guy from the video? Alright then, joker, go on in."

"Thanks…I guess. This guy here is my guest if that's okay."

"Sure, maybe he will be the next week's reel."

"Sorry dude," Bart retorted dryly. "The spotlight is something I'm fond of avoiding. Drinks are more my thing, if that's okay with you."

"Long as you don't make a scene. Don't care if it's for clicks or cash, we don't get paid if we let drunks go wild."

"It's all cool, dude, I swear that's not my thing."

Raul shrugged before he motioned for the two men to enter. Kevin and his friend did just that, and moments later they stepped through to see dozens of extremely attractive men and women dancing all around.

Bart took one glance at some of the women in front of him before he whistled. 'Damn, at the very least you were not lying about the sales pitch. Well, might as well figure out what drink to start out with. What about you, man?"

Kevin looked around and spotted Alison's friend Teri talking with a few people before he took a deep breath. "Well, my plan is to find Alison, see where things stand with her, then talk with Carlos. Nothing else really matters now.

"That girl over there, Teri, was friends with her in school. I think Alison said she was staying at her house while she was here. Guess they came together, and if I can't find Alison then I guess her friend is a good place to start."

"And I thought you were sober? Whatever, bro, let's get this party started."

Kevin saw Bart flash another laid back half-lopped smile before he took a deep breath and pressed through the crowd. After turning around for half a minute, he got to Teri just as she was going for food.

Teri saw Kevin walk up before she smiled. "Oh, hey you! I'll take some nachos, please!"

Kevin winced and chuckled as he scratched the back of his neck. "Sorry but I'm *not* a waiter. Teri, it's me, Kevin Summers. We had classes in high school together. . . remember? And, before that we were both friends of Alison?"

Teri blinked a few moments before she giggled. "Oh wow, Kevin, it really is you! Sorry, you had more. . . um. . . well you dressed a lot different than when we were in school and with the lighting you look like, um, someone else?"

"Well I was trying to look different than back then. Just. . . not trying to look out of place."

"I totally get that. I had to get very precise details from Ali on what will get a good response from some of her stud co-workers. I mean it's been one wild ride but got to make sure it ends with a bang. I mean, if I can score a night with a model, I will be less bummed when Alison leaves."

"I know the feeling. It's been a roller coaster, huh? Sad it seems like it's ending but got to make the most of it."

Bart snorted as he took a drink. "Long as you know when to get off the ride so you don't get burned, dude."

Teri eyed Bart carefully before she cleared her throat. "Wait, you don't work here, do you? Sorry, you look familiar."

"I used to work here for like, a few months, but you might remember me because I graduated the same year as you and Kevin, though we were not in the same circles. Bart's my name, don't play it out."

"No last name?"

"No offense but if we are too drunk to remember it, might as well keep it simple, right?"

"Hah, well I don't know if you were this funny back in high school but you're a blast now, Mister Bart. You trying to be a comedian?"

"No, just improved my humor while working in jail."

"Oh, wow you are trying to be a stand up?"

"That was not a joke. I did work in a prison half of last year while roaming around trying to find a place that did not suck. Well, it did suck but it got me to see working for Amazon most nights as a *less* sucky job."

"Oh, you got stuck with the night shift?" Teri blurted out. "That sucks!"

"I like it that way!" Bart proudly retorted. "Pays better and I don't have to deal with people who are pain in the asses, which is most people to be blunt."

"Tell me about it. Sounds like you have seen a lot of stuff, Bart. Any fun stories?"

"Maybe, but rather tell them while sitting down so I don't have to worry about losing my drink."

"Sure!"

Kevin saw Teri looked amused before he chuckled. "Are there any spare tables? Should we find Alison so we can talk together?"

"Hah, good luck with that, Kevin, Ali's been alongside Chandler all night talking with big-shots the whole party. It was mostly inner circle stuff to me."

"Chandler…I don't think I met him yet. Is he like that Carlos guy?"

"Oh, I think he and Alison are a *lot* closer."

Kevin felt a lump in his throat before he winced. "Oh, wait you mean this Chandler is her boyfriend?"

"I mean; I think they've known each other since Alison started working at Starlight. He might have even been the one who helped her get the job. I mean, I don't know if they're officially a couple, but the way they act maybe they don't need to bother with formalities."

Kevin grasped the table tightly and he was still for a few moments before he smiled. "Oh, I did not realize that. Well, guess it can be a fun time. Maybe they are busy, I'll just see if they are around."

Bart saw the look his friend had before he cleared his throat. "What you thinking of, buddy? Don't go trying some stunt like what you tried with that Samantha chick, man, I reckon it will blow up even worse this time around."

Kevin suddenly had a solemn look in his eyes as he looked down. "Don't worry Bart, I'm not stupid. I'm not going to bark up the wrong tree, just want to see what the state of said tree is. At the very least, just want to see where things stand either way before it's over. You guys find a spot. I'll be back."

Kevin walked towards the stairs to the upper level. Bart sighed. "Well…I would go with him, but I don't think he would like what I would have to say. Sell it to me straight, girl, is Kevin a friend to your pal or is it just a one-sided thing?"

Teri looked down for a few moments before she shrugged. "I mean, she *did* say she was happy to see him again when we have been hanging out. I mean, she won't talk much about him, or Chandler either. She likes hearing about my life but does not like talking much about her own aside from business."

"So, another one that has problems being honest? Maybe the two have more in common than I thought. Whatever, I'm not Doctor Phil. That's something they all got to figure out. But I'm down to talk about the top ten times I got ripped off by one boss or another if you're up for it."

"Sure, sounds like a good story," Teri said. Kevin nodded at the two and made his way to the upper level. He saw some of the models that worked with Alison, but not Alison herself. Just as he was starting to wonder if she was even on the floor, he heard a giggle and turned around to see Cammy walking by.

He saw she was looking a little flush but seemed amused. He cleared his throat. "Oh, hey there Cammy, hope you're enjoying the party."

Cammy rolled her eyes before she leaned back. "You don't think the show is still going on, do you? Our exchange is over, and your services are no longer required. Don't think you can get some extra footage."

Kevin saw her look of contempt and tried not to be phased as he just responded by laughing anxiously. "Oh, of course I would not try to get more work at a party and all. Well sorry for bothering you, I was just looking for Alison."

Cammy looked at Kevin for a bit before she giggled dismissively. "What, you don't think you can milk more stuff out of her, do you? *None* of us are doing overtime for you, got it?"

"I'm sorry if I gave the wrong impression, but I just wanted to talk with her. I mean, it might be a while till I talk to her again so just wanted to hang out with a friend one last time, right?"

"*Friend? Again* you say? You're even slower than I figured. Kevin, right? Alison is *very* busy talking with people that *matter*. Unless your conversation somehow matches that importance, I'm sure a text will suffice. After all, online conversations have replaced trivial conversations these days. To be blunt, the highlight of having these new ways of talking is to reduce face to face time with those that don't *deserve* that time."

Kevin could see the raw contempt in her eyes before he chuckled anxiously. "Well I mean, it's not as important as high-level stuff like that, of course. I can wait a bit, but I just hope we can have a good night."

"Look, you bumbling buffoon, wake up! You clearly twisted things in your head, but the reality is there is not much more for you to say to Alison than any other of the locals. You can't even comprehend how busy professionals are, don't push for more than you deserve."

"Is that what she said?" Kevin countered as he tried to restrain himself. "I don't know how much Alison told you, Cammy, but we go way back so…"

"You think that means *anything* now? Time may have not changed much for you, but she's in a different world than someone like you now. If you do care for her do her a favor and don't drag her into your buffoonery. After all, being the buffoon of the week may be the best heights the likes of you can reach, but Alison is someone who has a *much* brighter future in store, and it won't be delayed cause some nobody can't take a hint!"

Kevin saw some of the others to his side were chuckling at him before he winced. "So, you saw the video too, huh? That—that was out of my control. I know it's not very flattering, but I'm sure people like you must know all about things outside your control!"

"Oh, I'm very aware of there being two sides to a story, Kevin. But there are no two sides here. No, just one side that is a desperate façade that's trying to be maintained at all cost, and the sad, droll reality of a nobody. Let's be real, you're a man in your early thirties whose crowning achievement is being in a job fit for high school students on their summer breaks."

Kevin looked a little flustered as he tried to not lose his cool. "I get that my life's not what most would call ideal at the moment, okay? I'm trying to do what I can, there's a thing as late bloomers right?"

"And you think Starlight will help you bloom? Well, I suppose that's our mantra, but there has to be *some* talent to work with. You just don't have the talent to be on the same stage as someone like Alison. Your kind keeps thinking if you *just* get your chance in the spotlight, if you can get noticed, it can all work out. Don't you get that it's not that no one can see you, it's that we *do* see you and you're an unappealing eyesore to look at! After all, if you were a true genius, you would have figured out how to break out by now! You're not the worst of your kind, but you're clearly not special enough to deserve being in the limelight."

Kevin stared solemnly at the ground for a few moments before he looked up and asked, "So according to you I'm not good enough to be friends with people like you and Alison?"

"Just think about it for a second. What do you have to offer her other than holding her back with mundane desires? What can you really do for her that others can't? You think sharing the same childhood experiences matters *that* much?"

Kevin had memories of all his failures flash by before he grasped his hand tightly. "I get it, alright!? There are plenty of people better than me. It's been drilled into my head when I see everyone on TV, the people that everyone wants to see, don't look like me. It's been made quite clear, no matter what I put on my dating profiles on the websites, that I'm passed over because of how I look and what I write! But still, even still, I'm not just a joke, I'm still a person that has value!"

"And you think just because you exist that means Alison and the rest should want to date you by default?"

"I—I did not say that. I just…"

"Oh please, you give yourself too much credit. Even if that's not what you say, women like us know that's what guys like you really think deep down, we can see it in your pathetic eyes! You think every man deserves their dream girl no matter what? Despite what

Hollywood thinks, you don't get a 'soulmate' just out of pity."

"I know that, damn it. I don't think I deserve everything for nothing. I just don't want to die alone, alright? I just have to prove I'm good enough for..."

"For her? Good enough to be loved? You know back in the old days, women who could not be courted were seen as failures and the poorer ones were forced to live their lives alone as nuns because that's the path God chose for them. Was it fair? Did not matter, that's what everyone with power decided they deserved! But you men *never* thought the roles would be reversed.

"But despite how much some of you have been moaning about it, times have changed, women no longer have to settle for the Bronze. Only a little while ago, ladies had to settle for okay guys because they were not as bad as those around them.

"But with the internet, now people can find who is best suited from them even if they are across the world. Too bad for you and your kind, but that means you can't cheat the natural order anymore, you will take what you deserve, or you will get *nothing*. So now it's your turn to be the person that has to spend their life isolated and alone. Even if you yourself have not done anything wrong, its karmic justice for your kind!"

Kevin saw Cammy's pure hateful glare before he stepped back and tried to take her outburst all in. "Geez Cammy, what did I ever do to you?"

"You think you've done nothing? It's that clueless line of thought that pisses me off most of all! It's you and your kind still having the nerve to not see how times have changed. It's people like you who thought your regurgitated movie lines were clever enough for us to think we were worth your time!

It's having to go through so much because you thought you deserved affection! I'm sick of entitled brats yearning for what they don't deserve. Just admit you were wrong, you're an eyesore! You know how many times ladies such as Alison and I get hit on by worthless eyesores like you? You know how much of our time is bogged down by deranged losers who think it's their divine right to be loved for no reason? You really thought that just by doing work a trained monkey could do she would swoon over your face?"

Kevin was frozen as he was overwhelmed at Cammy's speech, and only felt worse as he realized there was some logic to what she said. He stuttered a few words before he just looked down. "I—I just, liked when I talked with Alison, that's all."

"Oh, I'm sure, but did you ever think how much Ali enjoyed talking to *you*?"

Kevin winced again, but before he could say something suddenly a new voice cut in with, "What about me, Cammy?"

Kevin saw that it was none other than Alison, who seemed to have just emerged from the bathroom. He saw she was dressed in jeans and a stylish purple blouse. Alison saw Kevin's look and flashed a smile. "Oh, hey Kevin. When did you get here? You okay? You…liking the party?"

Kevin almost responded instantly but caught himself after the first syllable. He saw Cammy's cold look and could not help but have even more memories of all the women that turned him down and kept thinking about what Cammy said about why Alison would pick him over others and realized he could not think of an answer. He just looked down and grasped his hands tightly. "Hey Alison, just wanted to see how you were doing."

Alison saw Kevin looked troubled before she raised an eyebrow. "Why? Is something wrong? Sorry Kevin, I have a lot going on tonight."

"That's fine, I know you're busy. I'll be quick. I… I just wanted to say I was glad we could catch up. I know it's been a while since we saw each other and that you have a lot more going on than me, but I just wanted to say despite everything, thanks for still seeing me as a person.

"I know that might sound like a no brainer, but after so many years of people either just treating me like I'm invisible, or just pretended they cared just to rip me off and then throw me out, it was nice that someone still cared enough to treat me like I mattered, even a little bit.

"I'm just glad you did not become one of those elitist snobs. I'm glad you're still you. Just hope you still remember me even for a little bit when you're the next superstar, Alison. Sorry, I know I took up enough of your time already, have a good night."

Alison was shocked to see Kevin take off so quickly and called after him. Her voice did not reach across the music, and people already blocked her from seeing him.

Alison saw Cammy looked relived before she narrowed her eyes at her. "Cammy, did you say something? Oh god, you're drunk already? You did not give Kevin the same kind of speech you gave Apu last year?"

"Oh of course I didn't Ali, cause *this* one was on purpose. No worries, just told the facts. Sure, I may have been blunt, but it was to drive the point home. It's for his own good, he seems to have made a fool out of himself enough as of late."

Alison realized Cammy was talking about the online video before she looked remorsefully at her own phone. "Cammy, you know that was his father acting out, not him, right?"

"Does it really matter? The sins of the father and all."

Alison grit her teeth at the remark as she thought of memories of her own father and other experiences with her family. She flicked her hair out of her eyes while snapping back with a sore, "Damn it, Cammy, we don't always follow in the footsteps of our family. I sure as hell did not."

Cammy was taken aback by Alison's sudden agitation before she cleared her throat. "Oh, come now dear, you don't think I was implying *you're* the same as him, do you? Of course not, I know your mother was a very classy lady that was just hoodwinked by your two-faced father. It's happened to us again and again across our history, that's why we have to make them pay for how they wronged us!"

"Oh come on, Cammy," Alison retorted as she rolled her eyes. "I know men screwed you, me and so many others but we can't blame Kevin for the sins of all men, it's—it's not right. Kevin's not that one crazy deranged fan who ambushed you, or Marco or anyone else that wronged you, at the very least don't lump him in with what others did!"

"Maybe, but still it's better to shut him down now before he acts on some deluded thought. C'mon Ali, it was clear as day he was pining form the moment he saw you back in this hovel of a town. You did not want him to ruin everything, did you?"

"Of…of course not," Alison answered with remorse. "But even if he had to see reality, it didn't have to be done so harshly. He's not acting like a crazy stalker. He's been polite, has not overstayed his welcome, and tried to be a part of the team."

"He's *tried* to fit in, Ali, but managing to not ruin things when you don't bring anything to the table does not really balance things out. Besides, that video shows his true nature. I hear from some of the crew he geeks out about *Star Wars* and all that nerd crap when he's talking with the other crew. He's trying to put up a mask, but his true nature seeps out when he thought no one was looking."

Alison winced as she looked back. "C'mon Cammy, talking about *Star Wars* is not like talking about doing creepy things, right? We *all* have different sides we show to different people, it's not that bad to talk about different things long as it's not harmful."

"True Ali, unless it's all just a pathetic facade. I know he does not seem as bad as some of the others, but it's clear as day this was his last desperate hope that things could go upward in his life. He's going to blow it as soon as he realizes dreams don't come true, so might as well have the bomb blow up without anyone else going down with him, right?"

Alison saw how driven her co-worker looked before she felt disgust building up inside her. "Enough Cammy! Kevin's not just some piece of trash to throw away! You can't just treat him like his life's been written out like a script! He's tried his best to be a friend. I want to make sure he will be okay when this ends. I should see if he's still here."

Alison was about to take off when she heard, "Whoa there dear, that *might* be a bad call." Alison felt a tug on her shoulder and turned around to see Chandler behind her. He gave a wide smirk before he looked around. "After what Carlos said, I figured it would be smiles all around, love. Don't tell me some party crasher is being a pain."

"No, not that," Alison answered. "Cammy kind of came down too hard on Kevin so I wanted to make sure he was okay."

"Your heart's in the right place, love, but that would be a mistake. Showing him *any* compassion would give him false hope. Best he's looked at by a neutral party, and I'll *gladly* fulfill the role."

Alison saw Chandler's grin get even larger before she raised an eyebrow. "Really? But have you and Kevin even met face to face yet?"

"Not at all, which is why it's as far from personal as it gets. C'mon, you know I'm good at calming people down! Remember when I got those union workers in Madrid to concede they were wrong? You don't need to do overtime, I'll make up for arriving late and make sure things are square with your long-time fan."

Alison saw Chandler looked excited, pondered the offer for a few moments before at last nodding, "Just, make sure he's all right, okay?"

"No worries, love. I'll make sure things are as they should be. Just put this behind you. Carlos and I talked with the higher-ups and after this they just might have a higher spot in the pecking order for you. Your future's about to soar to new heights, no need to waste time on the worthless baggage of the past. Have fun ladies. I promise this won't take too long. And when I get back the *real* fun can begin."

Chandler kissed Alison on the cheek and then left to find Kevin. Cammy saw the doubt on Alison's, she cleared her throat. "It will be over one way or another, Ali. Just focus on what's important so we all can get the futures we deserve."

Alison paused for a moment before she nodded. "It would be nice to at least move forward with life, long as it's the right way."

Alison followed Cammy to see the rest of her co-workers, and as she moved high, her childhood friend moved low.

***

Kevin was still processing all that happened and could barely keep himself from bumping into anyone and getting more attention. Too upset to gather his thoughts enough to go find Bart, he just made his way to a spot at the counter. The bartender saw him and said. "Damn man, looks like you can use a heavy ass drink."

"Just. . . water please."

"You sure, man? Look like you could use a *lot* more than water."

"I'm very sure. The last thing I need is to not be able to hold my feelings in right now."

The bartender saw the sullenness in Kevin's eyes and cleared his throat. "That's the case, dude? Well the customer is always right and all that. Just let me know if you want anything else."

Kevin nodded as he glanced at the water. He sat motionless as he thought over everything that happened since Alison returned, before the most recent memories he had flashed by and he grasped the glass tightly. "Damn it, at this point I don't know if anyone can give me what I want. Well, maybe God if he's generous about throwing out a miracle, something tells me I should not hold my breath."

He was about to wonder if he could eat without throwing up, then he heard a sly chuckle from behind. "I don't know mate, if your relying on God to bail you out, you're sounding *mighty* desperate."

Kevin looked around to see the high-ranking Starlight employee flash a smirk before raising an eyebrow. "Sorry, do I know you?"

"Nah mate, but I sure know you. You've been working with us on our gig here, right? Kevin Summers?"

Kevin eyed Chandler in confusion before he rubbed his head. "Sorry, have we met during the shoot? Sorry if I don't have your name memorized, it sometimes takes me a few times to get things memorized, and it's been a busy week."

"Oh no worries, mate, you have not seen me, but I sure have seen you, thanks to Alison. You can call me Chandler, Kevin."

Kevin's eyes widened as he saw how confident the man looked before he cleared his throat. "Alison's friend? I think she talked about you. You guys have been friends since she started working at Starlight?"

"A little off there, wanker, we were friends even before that and *I* got her the job. Don't want to brag but the simple truth is I have a *little* bit of pull, Kevin, if you're not used to it, it's what happens when you're someone important, someone with power."

Kevin winced as he saw how confident the man in front of him looked before he said. "Oh, is that so? Well, thanks for helping Alison get this far, glad she's doing so well. And if you are the one that helped her get the job, guess its thanks to you that we were able to meet again, even if it was only for a little while."

"Ah well, none of us are God so we can't see everything, chap. Sure did not think this would be more then another job for Alison, but guess more of her past popped up than we figured. But I guess some are just stuck in the past, or are just, unable to move on at all."

Kevin winced as he saw Chandler's tone sharpen and looked at his glass. "Well, like you said, we can't see the future, we can't see how things will unfold. But just got to live on and grasp the happy moments when you can."

"Not bad words, Kevin, though you're forgetting that sometimes we delude ourselves into thinking we can grasp what we don't deserve. That looks, rather unattractive, right, mate?"

"What do you mean? Did Alison say something? If I did anything that offended her, I'm sorry."

"Glad you're aware of how you affect those around you Kevin, that makes it easier. Would be a tad difficult if I had to drill the point home to some invalid. But since you're just subpar it will make this smoother."

"What do you mean?"

"Kevin, mind coming with me to talk? I assure you, it will make things *much* better for Alison."

Kevin's eyes widened as he looked around. "Oh, Alison wants to talk to me?"

Chandler saw how hopeful Kevin looked and snickered as he got up. "Well let's say this is her message, mate. Come now, the quicker we get this done the better for all of us. Here Barkeep, an extra tip for your troubles."

Kevin saw Chandler casually throw a fifty-dollar bill at the bartender. The man saw Chandler's grin and shrugged before taking it.

Kevin was uneasy as Chandler motioned for him to follow but remembered how he wanted to not make things worse for Alison. After a moment of looking for either Alison or Bart, and not seeing anyone, he followed.

It did not take long till the two exited the building and were at one of the parking lots. A few people were outside, but they were in the distance. Kevin looked around in confusion before he blurted out, "Oh? What's out here?"

"Just wanted to make sure you could hear me clearly, Kevin. Now then, be a good sport and show me you deleting her phone number and Facebook profile and anything else that could be used to contact her. *Just* so we can make sure this little part of our lives is over for good."

Kevin felt a lump in his throat as he blinked to make sure he heard right. "Come again? You want me to delete *all* ties I have to Alison? Why? I know she's leaving, but we are still friends."

"Come on mate, don't be difficult about this. Maybe you didn't think about it this way, but let me make it clear to you that Alison's never going to return to her past again. That means she will never revisit *anything* unprofitable again and she will have a easier time with less nobodies swarming around her like maggots that take away from her grace.

"Sorry to say, a washed up nobody is as unprofitable as it gets, so just make this easy and erase any connection you have to her. After all, further contact with you is nothing but a burden."

Kevin started to grit his teeth as he saw Chandler's smirk. "Damn it, if this is really what Alison wants, I want to hear it from her. I don't know you enough to trust you at your word."

"As Alison's boyfriend, I do have the privilege to speak for her. Frankly, you're in no position to argue here, mate, so comply or this will get even worse for you."

"So you and Alison are a couple? I've never seen anything to prove that!"

"Please...we don't need such trivial things such as a Facebook confirmation and shallow tripe like that when we are a natural couple. Our chemistry, the way we are in sync, it's as ideal a match as Adam and Eve. You're not really going to be a green-eyed sore loser, are you?

"After all Kevin, how can you possibly be a better match for her than me? I'm rather well off, charming, *and* can get things done. To be blunt, you're a product past its sell date. It's all downhill from here for you as you just decay more and more, have less and less to offer with each passing moment."

Kevin used all of his willpower to not lose his cool as he stepped forward. "Damn it, I get it, alright? I get why someone like you might be a better match for her in theory, but that doesn't mean I don't have the right to be friends with her!"

"Oh of *course* it does, you pathetic wanker, you just refuse to see it. People of higher status are weighed down when they are tied down to riffraff such as you. Just submit and accept your place, and you just *might* find some peace in acceptance."

"Damn you!" Kevin seethed out as he got in front of Chandler's face. "You arrogant bastard, it's one thing when you have everything lined up for you, but do you have any idea how horrible it is when you're missing so many things in your life and someone tells you to just be content with what you have?"

"Looking mighty spoiled there, Kevin. After all, you still have more than most in the Middle East will ever get and all."

"I know that, damn it. Call me being the glass half full kind of guy all you want, but even if I'm not the worst-off person alive, it does not mean I'm content with nothing *ever* getting better! America was *supposed* to be a place where if you worked hard your dreams come true. So many people called me lazy over the years, but I tried as hard as I could!

"But one thing after another, things ended up in a dead end! Journalism, radio, history, damn it, everything that's not related to business, sports, and tech became a dead end! But no matter how hard it took to make your dreams come true, it was not supposed to be like this, damn it."

"I'll give you some slack, Kevin," Chandler retorted wryly. "Back before everyone thought the world was going to end because of Y2K and all that nonsense, you could pass that every kind of person could do well if they just gave it their all.

"The good old American Dream has lasted for centuries because it's a damn good sales pitch! I mean who would really take 'you will take your portion of gruel and like it' over working your ass off to make life what you make it and all that?

"But alas, computers just about crushed that dream for the lot of ya. If I'm being nice, maybe if things were as they were when you first had your dream you could have been someone, somewhat respectable, but alas, time does not stand still just because you wish it, and in the end that world just does not exist anymore.

"Don't feel too bad, mate, the truth is that as much as society does not want to admit it, the middle class is all about to slip away. The new American dream, this American Tango is all about two steps forward, one step back. If you're fast, you can skip ahead of the riffraff, but otherwise you're going to fall behind.

"We are just about going back to the old days, where things were simple, and there was only the leader, the nobility, and the rabble. The way the world is now, artists are only able to have a pleasant profitable life only if a patron of importance likes them, talent's really just secondary, to be blunt.

"Because in the end art, history, journalism, that's all just trivial in the face of careers that have *real* power. Yes…banking, programming, the world is transitioning to where only jobs that have real power bring prosperity, and everyone else must submit to where they are in the caste system.

"But to be honest it's even more simple than that. With machines enabling us to purge professions that have become redundant, mate, those who have value now are only those who can do what machines can't, and that's those who have charisma.

"Charisma was always vital, but now it is *everything*. Now it does not matter really what you want to do, be it being a cook, a star athlete, or even a respected plumber, in the end if you can't get a good social media following you have no chance, because that shows who is a winner in today's world, and who is a loser.

"Does not matter if you uncovered who killed President Kennedy and made contact with chummy aliens, people will still pick listening to a charismatic man talk about his beer over you if they like how he looks and sounds talking about it over your stale dribble.

"In the end, the past century has really been a glitch in the natural order. Everything was going so fast that artists, journalists and all the others were able to pull all these things to make *far* more money than they deserve. But the elite just about got the chain back on the beast that is the internet and things just about are aligning to how they *should* be. Now those with charisma are without a doubt the elite, and those without it are at the bottom, as it should be.

"I admit, I'm just where I am because of my family and the skills to know how to feel the room, but in the end that's all that really matters in life, right? Alison belongs with me, Kevin. If you had what it took to impress a lady of her calibre you would have already pulled it off.

"But since you're here, just know your place before whatever you can get slips out of your grasp. Just accept the likes of you should just find some fellow average gal. You might not really love her, and she might not really love you, but you're the kind who will have to settle for being with anyone that can put up with someone so subpar. So, it's either compromise or the loneliness, chap.

"If you just accept where your place is you just might feel better. After all, even if it was at your expense, you do provide quite a lot of laughter for people like a proper jester. I knew people would eat up such buffoonery the moment I saw that pitiful display."

Kevin's eyes widened as he took in what Chandler implied, and his jaw dropped. As it all set in, he turned beet red. "Wait…it was *you* who put up that video! You…you made a laughingstock out of me! Alison, if she knew…"

"She was there when I sent the video, Kevin," Chandler said. At seeing Kevin's shock, the other man's grin widened. "Oh yes…it may have not been her most blissful moment, but she had no qualms with me submitting the footage. After all, it is the *only* way someone like you can be noticed. You should thank me mate, at least you looked good being a fool, as good as a fool can!"

"Damn it, am I just a joke to you!?" Kevin seethed with fury as veins formed on his forehead. "You think my life's just some punchline for the likes of you? Damn it, I'm not just a joke!"

Kevin could not help himself as he formed a fist. He was about to strike Chandler, who merely smirked. "Easy now, mate. You sure you want to do this? You think striking me will do anything but prove you're a petty scum, and prove to Alison, and every other girl, you're an unstable wild dog that should be put down?"

Kevin froze at that, and as he wondered if Alison was watching, Chandler's grin widened, before he slugged Kevin in the chest with a swift right hook. Kevin felt a surge of pain powerful enough to slam him into the building's logo on the wall, then fell to the ground.

As he gasped for breath, Kevin saw Chandler in a boxing stance, looking smug. "I'm no savage, but I *did* take boxing class seriously, precisely so I could keep rabble in check. You tried hard, mate, I can see that. But in the end your base nature reveals itself and you *must* pay for trying to fool your betters."

Chandler unleashed a swift kick to Kevin's jaw to smash him into the ground. As Kevin coughed out blood, Chandler kicked him in the gut. "Maybe this will drill the point that someone like you should never reach beyond your station again! It's so obvious someone like you will blow up sooner or later. What other destiny does a dead end loser like you have? Might as well defuse the bomb before you drag anyone else down in flames as well. Now, delete all contact info on Alison and maybe I'll decide not to press charges for assaulting me."

Kevin saw a glass wine bottle discarded behind the car he was next to and grasped his fist angerly as his frustrations boiled over. ". I'm not a joke. I'm not a joke! Damn it…you can't get away with this!"

"Course I will, I'm far richer than you and everyone in your family combined, mate. My father could buy everything in this town and there would be nothing any of you could do about it. Like I said, we are back to old school ways mate, to the lords and the peasants! And peasants who can't understand their station will…"

"Hey what's going on over there, dude?"

Kevin saw that three random local men noticed what was going on and headed over. Chandler saw they looked alarmed before he said. "Nothing to worry about gents, just a dispute that's being settled right about now."

The tallest of the men raised an eyebrow and saw how miserable Kevin looked. Kevin looked at the broken glass bottle for a few moments, saw everyone looking at him, and just moaned in despair.

The men saw the pure misery on Kevin as he lay on the ground nearly moaning like a wounded animal before the one in the middle narrowed his eyes. "Hey, that's the guy on the local news, right? Man, I think he's had enough. Doesn't look like he's a threat."

"To your eyes maybe, but he's the type that needs to have the message drilled in so he *never* makes the same mistake again."

"That's not your call, dude! I don't like that smile, so back off before we have a problem."

"Careful mate, touch me and you're going to be buried in lawsuits. I can sue everyone in town at once and come out on top, so stand down. Don't mean to make this a scene, I spent enough time with this as it is. So, this should wrap up everything, right Kevin? Just be a good mutt and stay out of sight, where you belong.

"If not, I'll sue you and no matter what lawyer you would hire, you will be buried in fees regardless of the outcome. Just embrace your life and you will find peace, Kevin. Or, at least you will see your place in life clearly. I don't really care as long as I *never* see you again."

Chandler snickered as he swept some dust off his shirt and walked back inside. The three guys looked at each other before they walked up to Kevin. 'You okay, dude? That smart-ass break anything?"

"No…nothing new is broken," Kevin said as he got back to his feet. The guys around him all looked at each other before the shortest one raised an eyebrow. "You sure we should not call someone, dude?"

"Thanks, really, but at this point just want this to end. I just need to walk it off."

"Well, if you say so, man. Should we go get someone inside?"

Kevin paused for a moment as he staggered back. "There's no point, there is no one inside that would care. Thanks for caring."

Kevin gave a weak wave before walking off. He staggered forward like a zombie, almost on instinct just wanting to get away from what happened. Kevin tried to think of what to do next as his vision felt foggy because of the blow he took.

As he stops to think, he realized at that moment, he had no idea what to look forward to, only things to dread, only pain. He let out a short yell of frustration, kicked a can and saw it go down the nearby bridge.

He looked down at the water and saw a reflection of a car parked next to it. The sight of himself caused a pulse of revulsion to vibrate across his body as he felt despair creeping down his spine. He coughed up more blood as he fell to his knees. He was about to say something when he noticed an old man walking past him.

The older male looked dishevelled, and seemed to not even notice Kevin, walking nearly like a zombie himself, aimlessly walking to find purpose. Kevin saw the old man mumble something as he walked forward and looked at himself.

Is…is this all I have to look forward to in life? To cling on in misery, stumbling around in despair? I tried so hard, but am I fated to be like my uncle, because that's all my family can amount to?

Damn it, damn it all! As much as I hate that smug jackass, I hate even more that I don't have anything to really counter his point. I feel so worthless, because it's clear in the eyes of so many I'm already just a worthless joke, and I don't know a damn thing about what to do about it! Damn it!

Kevin grasped his head, still throbbing after hitting the logo, and cried out, unable to feel anything but numbing pain.

11

---·~❧⚜❧~·---

The Strength to Gaze into a Sincere Reflection

While Kevin's world was collapsing, Alison was worried about him in the back of her mind, but still mostly focusing on the business ventures she could realize by the end of the night.

After she saw Kevin and Chandler go out, she and Cammy went up to join Carlos. He was with many of her fellow models, and a few other Starlight personnel who were all celebrating getting another gig done. Bright and Sam were there to celebrate.

Alison arrived in time to see Bright and Carlos toast each other's wine glasses together as Bright blurted out, "Well Carlos, thanks for a job well done. Been working for a lot of big fish who think they can just thrash around our pond here and expect everyone to dance to their tune. That's why it's always a pleasure to deal with folks that still remember what business etiquette is."

"Can't speak for everyone but where I'm from work bonds are a matter of pride, Bright," Carlos said as the two exchanged handshakes. "Starlight may be well full of stars, but it does not mean we forgot what makes stars, or cocky enough to think stars are the only ones that matter. Trust me, I know all about how much it takes a crew to make their star look good. Glad you guys got something out of it too, Bright."

Bright thought about Kevin before he winced and chuckled again. "It would seem that everyone got something different out of it, but that's life. Our town got some good ratings out of it at least. Only a handful of DVD sells but hey, digital streaming's where it's at, Carlos. I may be on my way out but I'm going to be on top of the game till I throw in the towel.

"Still...I guess some of the others still might have more to climb.... hopefully. That being said.... think any of the others might have a place in your biz full time? I value my staff, but I know most of them can't make a livelihood just working part time."

Carlos's eyes hovered over his glass as he realized Bright was most likely referring to Kevin. Carlos cleared his throat before he said. "I'm sure you know it takes a lot to earn a full time gig these days, right Bright? Who knows, man, always a lot of possible outcomes after what we find in a shoot, yah know? But to be honest with you, it's too soon to confirm anything.

"After all, my head honcho is not here, but back in our HQ. And nothing major flies without their approval, you know? It's more than just new talent that's being graded man, it's our girls too. Fact is some of our Starlighters are being evaluated from this gig and depending on how they score they might be moving up."

Bright saw Alison blush before he raised an eyebrow. "That so? What, they scouting for the next Miss America Pageant? They still do American Idol these days, right? Just a lot of things have gone off the air last few years."

Alison cleared her throat before she flicked some hair out of her eyes. "That has happened to former Starlight members in the past, Mister Bright, but many also go on to the likes of Broadway and

Hollywood. Not everyone makes it, but of course you know that."

Bright saw Alison looked passionate before his smirk widened. "So that's your aim, huh, missy? Well, if that's your dream, I guess I don't need to tell you how many people want to be the next Jodi Foster or Julia Roberts or something and come up short, kid. I take it you've been in some indie films or something to build up your cred?

"Kevin gave up being a movie star when my pal Earl once outright told him that his face was only going to be cast for sidekicks and throw away bad guys, but he tried a few things here and there all the same."

Alison looked unsettled for a moment, before she cleared her throat. "Is that why you never gave him a paying job?"

"That's what he said?"

"No…I just saw you have him work for years…and he gets nothing for it. He says its experience, but if it never leads to anything is that not just stringing him along?"

To her shock Bright winced at that, before he chuckled bitterly." Guess you're an expert at that, right girl? Sorry, don't mean to get snippy, I guess I can see why you might see it this way. Still, you think it looks good on any company when their employees are stuck far longer than they should be?

"Honestly I wish I could pay Kevin by now, but business has not been in its golden years for a long time now. Frankly me and Sam do this when we could be retired and do it for the passion over the profit. There used to be others with us that were like Kevin, they all had to move far away just to be able to afford a roof over their heads.

"I know Kevin tries; I'd hire him if things were ideal, but it's just not. Still, I keep giving him jobs so he can keep having something to get him out of the house. Don't want to see him isolated so much he loses it. Saw it happen far too often these days, so just doing what I can to hold that off because, Kevin deserves better than that at least."

Alison was shocked seeing the regret in Bright's eyes, but just as she was about to respond a chuckle that oozed with confidence cut her off, "Noble aims for sure sir, but to be honest sometimes it's best to stop holding off the inevitable and let the chips fall where they may." Alison was shocked to see the person talking was Chandler. His collar was slightly crooked, and he had a wild, if not feral look in his eyes.

He puffed his chest up as he threw in, "Anyway you got it all wrong, mate. Ali is not going to be the next anyone, her stardom will shine to far greater heights because she will have *my backing*, and Starlight's!"

Bright and Sam looked at each other for a moment, but Alison saw the state Chandler was in and could not help but feel alarmed. "Chandler? What happened? Did you go to see Kevin?"

"Oh, it's sweet of you to be concerned love, but trust me, it's nothing to dwell on. The matter took as much time as a situation with people like him required. So enough about that. We've been delayed from the things that matter enough as it is. Yes, time we focus on both of our futures, Alison."

Alison saw some of the other models looked confused before she asked. "Chandler, have you been drinking? The higher-ups are still going over things."

"Have you forgotten I'm part of those higher-ups, Ali? And with some insider info, some not so little birdies might have chirped that based on your results, you're a candidate for an upcoming movie."

Alison's jaw dropped as she saw Cammy raise an eyebrow before clearing her throat. "Pardon? Since when was Alison even being *considered*? She's *still* too green!"

"Oh, don't flash those green eyes of jealousy, Cammy," Chandler quipped. 'I know you've been around longer, but Starlight's all about people reaching their full potential. But no matter how much we try, part of it is about being at the right place at the right time. I suppose it helped that I managed to have lunch with a few producers that were looking for something fresh."

Alison looked at Chandler with a mix of shock and awe before she staggered back. "What, what!? You seriously got me a role in a movie?"

"Thought I was all talk, love? It may not be the top billing yet, but it's something. I scratched his back and he scratched mine, as simple as that. Just going to see if we can sweeten the deal for the land here, and it will be wrapped up nice and tidy."

"Deal...what deal?" Alison said in confusion.

"Oh, it's not related to you, Alison, it's just the land deal with some apartments in the center of the town and what not."

Sam saw how casual Chandler was before he raised an eyebrow. "Hold the phone, son. You're working with those snakes trying to slam a bunch of overpriced luxury apartments right in the middle of town and get rid of one of our parks?"

Bright nodded before he grunted out," Damn it, we been trying to overturn them for years, but they are some hot shot Eastern European company trying to sink their teeth into American soil! If they pull it off, it will jam up the entire town and suck a ton of the town's funds around it!"

"Oh, come now Mister Bright, I thought you were a man of business? I know everyone's extra revved up about their roots these days, but all the fellas that are at the top of their game know that soon capital will replace borders.

"It's going to be the good old days of company towns, where it was really simple because the company decided *everything*. How did you think Starlight was going to help your town? Did you not realize they act as good showgirls to further entice possible buyers to well, *buy* the town and remodel it as they see fit? You did not think people would just give the town money with no strings attached, did you?

"You should get with the times, sir, not too late even for someone of your age. Otherwise, you guys will be as hopeless as Summers. After all, you already have a landlord, what's switching to another one when it's a better deal?"

Bright turned red as he cracked his neck. "Kid, I'll take your word that you know a thing or two about business, but I'm not going to let a guy who deals with fashion tell me how a town works!"

Carlos saw Sam and some of the other locals in the back looked agitated, he cleared his throat and said. "C'mon Chandler, ease up, amigo. I know you have your thing, but we are here about our gig, and that has nothing to do with it."

"Well, they are not *entirely* unrelated, Carlos. The locations our girls filmed served as demos for my good friend Yuriev to entice him to make his bid."

"The hell Chandler? When were you going to tell *me* that?"

"Ease up, mate, you're all not part of the process, so it was not something you had to be concerned with, simple as that."

Sam saw some of the others looking annoyed before he said. "Word to the wise, mate. If you don't want to rack up one hell of a turnover rate, you might want to be on the level with your team more than once in a blue moon."

Chandler slicked his hair back. "Don't take this the wrong way, but while I'm younger, I play a *far* bigger game than you guys have been playing your entire lives. And at the level I play at, the happiness of every one of my co-workers is not a luxury that can always be afforded. Sometimes, you have to cut your losses and cut off rotting limbs to get ahead."

Sam noticed blood on the younger man's shirt before he asked. "Guess you're really good at cutting."

As Sam pointed to the bloody parts of the other man's shirt, Alison saw the blood thanks to the extra lights and gasped in horror. "My god, what the hell happened, Chandler?"

He raised an eyebrow at the blood on his shirt before he gritted his teeth. "Damn wanker made more of a mess than I realized. No worries, love. Kevin was not really happy with his dreams imploding around him, but I made it quite clear where he stood. Was not glamorous, but it had to be done. Too bad for him he learned the hard way he will not just yell his delusions into reality. No pain...*no* gain, right?"

Bright eyed Chandler carefully before he cleared his throat. "Let's be really clear about this, Kevin punched *you?*"

"Spot on, mate. You might want to keep an eye on him, Bright. He's totally out of touch with reality and it's dislodging the screws in his brain! Just saying, better watch him closely before he blows up and takes everyone around him down too. Sorry Ali, your childhood chum's like a rabid dog at this point, better just leave him to rot. He might go postal if he sees you, and I'd hate to see you get in a pitch."

Alison was motionless during Chandler's entire explanation, and just looked at the blood carefully before she got right up to his face. "Chandler...*where* did Kevin hit you again?"

"Oh, he got a cheap shot on my cheek, but I quickly paid him back for it. Nothing savage, just enough to drive the point home. No worries, love. Nothing was damaged enough to hamper our night. C'mon lets..."

Chandler was in the process of putting his hand around her, but to his shock she suddenly threw his arm off her. Alison had a sudden harsh look form in her eyes as she backed up. "The way the blood is on your shirt, it's not *your* blood! It..it was Kevin's!"

"Oh, I don't know how many drinks you had, Ali, but let's not be silly now."

"Don't belittle me, Chandler! I've seen when people have had other people's blood on them enough to know how things look. Between that and your face, you were lying about Kevin! You hit him?"

"Don't be so sensitive, Alison. Fine if you want to be precise, I delivered the first physical blow, but between his words and his body language it was clear he was a rabid dog, so I struck before I got bit."

"Damn it, Chandler, that's just you cherry picking things!"

"That's all that matters, Alison! Why are you even wasting your breath defending that classless loser? It's what he'd…"

Alison slapped Chandler before he could finish. Chandler just looked on in shock before he slowly saw just how angry Alison was. He blinked for a few moments before he rubbed his sore cheek. "The hell is this for? I'm your boyfriend, and he's the washed up nobody!"

"So *now* we are an "official" couple? He may not be as successful as you are, Chandler, but he's *not* a nobody! If you're so threatened by Kevin, it's making me see just how insecure you really are. I hate when people assume things, and you're assuming we are more than how things are."

"You serious? I thought we had a good thing going, Alison?"

"I sure as hell know you enjoyed all our online chats. It's how we became such good partners that we were able to strike out even during the time that most saw it as a lost year! And it sure seemed like it's been fun at Paris, Rome, Madrid, Tokyo, and the rest of the good times we had on our tours!"

"I did, but what I don't enjoy is worrying that you're not honest with me. I told myself it was just part of the job with how you act with other women, but more and more I'm beginning to wonder if you're just stringing me along, like the others."

"Goddamn it, did Kevin whisper such doubts in your head? Don't let that *nobody* ruin everything, Alison. You and I both know that the nature of relationships is more fluid than how our parents use to think romance worked. I thought we understood that its foolish to think passion can only happen with one person all the time, and all that matters is sharing the same goals?

"Did coming back to your home get you infested with outdated ideas? I promise you you're someone I don't want to lose. You just can't let fools take advantage of your fears to misguide you! If I knew Kevin was confusing you this badly, I would not have let him off so easily."

"Kevin didn't do anything, Chandler! I've just been thinking about things, enough to rethink things I thought I didn't have to think about."

"Well then you're thinking wrong, Ali! You're on the path to becoming a superstar, what else is there to think about?"

Before she could answer a male voice cut in with, "*Maybe* she's thinking about having some pride, huh dude?"

Chandler paused as he saw the voice came from Bart. Bart and Teri had gone to get some more drinks when they saw Alison and Chandler were shouting. Chandler saw Bart flash a half-looped grin before his right eye twitched. "And who the hell are you? Mind your own business, mate, this matter does not concern you."

"Oh, I don't know, I hear you're punching people like you're posing to be in Fight Club, so I figured it might be my business."

"What do you mean? You're a cop or something?"

"Not quite, just a fella who finds it a drag when someone's going around slugging people. Just doing my part for the neighborhood, but I'm getting a vibe you're the kind of guy who passed on the whole neighbor thing, huh?"

"Don't butt your nose in where it doesn't belong, wanker! That fool got what he had coming to him!"

Bart paused before he nodded and sipped his drink. "Guess that makes sense. A man's got to pay his debts."

Chandler saw Bart turn around before he laughed. "Glad you

have some common sense. It's always better when people understand their … GUH!"

Chandler was cut off because when Bart had turned around, it was a feint to get the shorter man to lower his guard, allowing Bart to slug him hard with a lunging punch. The blow hit Chandler right in the jaw with enough force to knock him off his feet.

As Chandler landed with a thud, Bart cracked his neck. "Guess you paid yours, wanker. Kevin may run around with rose tinted glasses, but kicking a man when he's down sure is a way to piss me off."

Alison was too shocked at how suddenly things escalated to do anything but gasp. As she heard Chandler moan, she saw his phone was still on the table, and that an email with her name was on it. As she looked at it, Chandler moaned, before yelling in rage.

Chandler grasped his now bloody swollen face as he glared at his attacker. "That was the dumbest move you will have ever made, bastard! I'll make sure you *never* get a job in this town again!"

Bart just laughed as he cracked his neck. "No skin off my bones, I was thinking of mixing things up myself. One way or another this party's not really gelling with me, so I think I'll leave now that I've equalized things. Peace out."

Bart flashed a peace sign before walking away, as most were too dumbfounded and in shock. Chandler saw Bart laugh before he grit his teeth. "Damn it, Carlos, have the cops bury that scum! Just take his name from the guest list!"

Carlos cleared his throat before he looked down. "Sorry man, don't really know who that guy is."

Bright just shrugged as he leaned back. "That guy does not work for me either, so it's out of my hands. You know him, Sam?"

His co-worker paused before he shrugged. "Nope, first time I seen him myself."

Chandler nearly snarled in rage as he glared at the nearest security guard. "Well *someone* must know who he is! Who is he?"

The guard radioed in, waited a few seconds and broke the silence with a shrug. "Sorry, his name was not on the guest list."

"Damn it, then get the security cameras at the entrance!"

Bright chuckled as he leaned back. "Sorry about that, but there are no cameras in the entrance. You know how us small towns are with our limited funds and all that."

"God damn it, this backwater town is becoming more trouble than it's worth. That's it, let's depart, Alison. We have more important things to do than rot with the rest of this dying hobble."

Alison just kept her head down as she said, "Is that so? You mean like me acting as a stripper?"

Chandler saw Alison looked even more agitated than before and responded with restrained bewilderment. "Ali, I'm really not in the mood for outbursts brought on by drunken confusion."

He was cut off as Alison put his phone in front of his face. As he saw what email was on it, he winced as she seethed, "Oh I'm confused? Because it seems the person in this email is confused, because he said I'm the on-stage stripper for his film! You told me I was going to have a role, not be eye candy for the background!"

"I know this has been an emotional time, but don't act rash. You're not just in the background, you have a few sentences with the main lead…asking if he wants a lap dance."

Alison's eyes widened before she grit her teeth and walked up to Chandler. "Damn it, you think that will change much?"

"I'm sorry if I caused you to come to the wrong conclusion, Alison, but what were you expecting? You're not known for your acting, so you're lucky to get a line at all! Beggars can't be choosers!"

"I didn't really think I would just have a leading role handed to me, but if I was that desperate for attention, I would have tried being a porn star or something."

"Ali, it's true you deserve better, but we just have to work around things to get what we want! You have to trust me!"

"Is that so? Trust you, just like how your father trusts you to do something, but you're doing a deal differently behind his back?"

"Wh—what the hell are you? No, no you."

Alison stepped back before scrolling back to another email, one between Chandler and the Yuriev individual he talked about earlier. Chandler took a deep breath before he said, "Alison, it's improper to look through another's emails. You don't know what you're looking at. How did you get through all this so bloody fast?"

"I thought you knew that girls like us have to act fast to make progress? I was looking for other emails about my job and saw the name of the guy you were just talking about. Chandler, I knew you had to be aggressive to succeed in business, but undercutting your own father is pushing it."

"Damn it, Alison, don't meddle in things you don't understand! True, I'm not telling my father about *part* of the deal, but it's all to get around the bureaucrats and red tape that hamper things and secure an even better deal!"

Carlos winced as he looked at the phone. "Chandler...are you loco? You know your padre is sharp and will find out if you're going against what *he* wants."

"He will be proud I showed how driven I can be. He's been saying one must be ruthless to be a winner, and I'm showing him I can succeed him by being sharper than him.

"Alison, we were drawn to each other because we both admired each other's passion. You knew that it would not be a smooth ride, but you wanted something fun over something safe. That is, till that..."

"Kevin did *not* con me, Chandler!" Alison snapped back defensively. "It's just, seeing him and my hometown just got me to rethink things I had not thought of for a while. I have had doubts for a while now, seeing Kevin and everything else about my past just caused me to think about it more. I…I don't want to be a nobody, but I don't want to become the kind of person I hated growing up, like the person that turned my dad against my mom."

"Ali, it's a horrible time to be having second thoughts. If you get cold feet, you're *never* going to get a chance to reach the top again! Alison, I thought you had the stomach for success. Don't back down just because of some memories getting in the way."

Alison closed her eyes for a few moments. Just as Chandler was about to say something, she opened her eyes again with a look of blazing determination. "I want to succeed, but I want to succeed at being the person I want to do. I know I can find a way to go down that path."

Chandler eyed Alison with bafflement before he snorted in shock. "So, you're going to throw everything away to feel good about yourself, Ali? Confidence is dandy, but if you're just being blind about it, you're just going to be an even bigger fool than your childhood chump. So, are you going? What the hell?"

Chandler was cut off as his phone suddenly buzzed. He saw he had a call and turned pale as he saw his father was calling him. His eyes darted around as he saw his coworkers were all giving him uneasy looks before he gulped. "What, why, why would father be calling me now?"

"Maybe because I sent him a copy of the email between you and Yuriev and he *might* have a few things to say about it?" Alison said with a smirk. As Chandler's jaw dropped, she flicked her hair out of her eyes. "Who is the bigger fool again? If you're going to lie to me, Chandler, you don't have to answer to me. Still…when you made a promise to your old man you have to answer to him. Have fun. Carlos, I need to take care of something."

Carlos saw how determined Alison looked before he said. "Go for it, girl. I could use some air myself, but better make sure things don't blow up any more than they are."

Alison smiled at the response, and as Chandler yelled at his father, she looked out the window. She was shocked to see Kevin still leaning over the bridge. Even from the distance she could see he looked nearly dead in his eyes before she turned pale. *No...Kevin. Please, not like this.*

She quickly dashed out of the room as everyone else watched Chandler get more and more panicky at the loud voice coming from his phone.

***

For as much as things exploded at the top of the building, Kevin had not moved an inch since he came to the bridge.

He just looked at the water, seeing his reflection while grasping his still pounding head. Thinking of all the things he hoped for that did not come true, and how now he was unable to think of anything positive about the future. This caused the coldness in his stomach to feel worse.

Kevin realized his hand was shaking before he leaned down. "Now what? Should I just go back with Bart? And then...I'll have to go back to dad and say he was right. And then, it's just back to the same old, till I die? Life...really does feel like just one bad joke right now. If, this is all there is, if it's all downhill from here, then maybe it will make more sense in."

Kevin's musing was cut off as he suddenly heard an urgent, "Wait Kevin!"

Kevin froze as he blinked. He wondered if he was losing his mind, but upon hearing footsteps he turned around and saw Alison was running up to him.

Kevin saw his childhood friend looking stressed before he said. "Alison?"

She gave a few haggard breaths before she spoke. "Kevin, what do you think you're doing?"

Kevin saw how upset Alison looked and at once got fearful she was angry at him. Kevin was so stressed he tried to mumble something that came out incoherent and tripped over a soda can as he walked towards her.

It was not a hard fall, but as Alison walked forward, Kevin looked mortified as he kept his head down. "I'm sorry Alison, I'm sorry for everything. I—I should have known my place. I'm so sorry I caused trouble coming back into your life again. I promise I won't ever be trouble for you again."

Alison realized how shamed Kevin looked as he kept his head down. She shocked Kevin as she got on her knees besides him. "Kevin, I don't want that to be how tonight ends, okay?"

Kevin saw how sad Alison looked before he blinked in confusion. "So, your not mad at me for bothering you the whole time you been back?"

Alison took a deep breath, before she let out a sweet smile." Kevin, do, do you remember what I said when we first met? How, if you did not be rude to me, I would not be rude to you? I, I still see things that way, and I'm so sorry you thought otherwise."

Kevin saw Alison looked sincere before he blinked and dared himself to feel hopeful." You, you still remember that?"

"Course I do, silly. I mean, it's one of the first real promises I made to a friend. Kevin, I have changed a lot, but how I view friends, real friends, has not."

"Alison, thank you. So, you did not want Chandler to teach me a lesson? You did not want him to release the video?"

"No, I was not really on board. I'm sorry, I should have stopped him. I allowed myself to think that he was right and that it might help you, that it was the only way you could be noticed, because I allowed him to con me into thinking that was reality. I've been so used to him taking care of things mostly because I did not have to care who his actions affected. But I'm starting to realize we were not on the same page after all."

"So, you did not tell him and Cammy to say those things?"

"You really got thrown in the gauntlet and got chewed up tonight eh? I thought I did, but they were being far harsher than they needed to be. Kevin, seems like even before Chandler hit you, you've already been in pain for a while, right?"

Kevin looked down before he winced. "It's no big deal. It's…it's my own fault for not being good enough. I know all of this does not matter. Over the past…decade everyone made it clear to just shut up about how I feel because no one cares. I mean, everyone's friends die I guess, its nothing special."

"Wait, your friend died?"

"Well, yeah. You did not meet him. It was after you left. But the summer after you left, I met this guy named Marco. We liked the same things and he helped me feel better after you left. We were friends for years, but he got sick and died right when I went to college. They just could not figure out what was wrong with him in time and that was that.

"I knew other friends that just lost their minds from all the stress. I was not as close with them as I was with Marco but still, sucks when people you care about are suddenly either gone or so gone in the head they might as well be gone. But I know everyone has their stuff to go through, I know no one cares…all they care about is what you can do for them."

Alison saw how rehearsed Kevin's speech was before she put her hand on his shoulder. "I *do* care Kevin. It's okay…I know you been holding back to not make a big deal out of things, but you don't have to pretend to act like you're something you're not. You don't have to feel ashamed. I lost contact with people, but so far none of my friends have died. But I did lose my mother."

"Wait, she did die? I'm so sorry, I didn't know."

"It's okay, she changed her name after the divorce. I knew she was sick, but never came back to visit. I was mad at her for giving up on me, but I guess I never even gave her a chance. I just wanted to keep looking forward and not look back.

"But I wondered if I made the right choice, a lot. Truthfully, that's why I came back to Cecily's funeral. I may have skipped my mom's funeral, but at least I could be there for one of the people I still knew, like Emily. I thought about how much I gained, by throwing away what I had, and then I saw you were there for your mother when she was sick, giving up what you could have had.

"That's why I'm so sorry you had to go through that, Kevin. I have not had stuff like that happen to me, but I know how hard it can be to get over trauma, despite what people say. We all want to work hard, but sometimes it is just sheer luck who gets a lucky break or not.

"I know you feel inferior to guys like Chandler, but don't. I've seen plenty of people like you who have tried hard and just could not catch up because of things outside of their control. For a while I thought that people who were poor were just lazy, that they were not willing to work as hard as I have. But after reflecting over things I admit, it was more because Chandler wanted me around than me standing out over the others.

"As much as we hate to admit it, sometimes it is just about luck. But we've got to keep fighting until the right opportunity comes along. After all, we don't want our life to just amount to what it is now, right?"

"No, of course not!" Kevin responded passionately. "I—I just don't know how to get out. I'm sorry, I know I should be able to figure something out, but every time I find a lead it just turns out to be a mirage. I, at times I felt like I have been trapped in a maze, and every way out was just an illusion, or someone lying to me to rip me off before screwing me over. I, no, if I was better it would have led somewhere, it's my fault."

"Don't blame yourself for everything, Kevin, it's not healthy," Alison answered softly as she squeezed his right hand. "You've just got to keep trying, no matter how long it takes. You know how they say girls can see when a man is desperate?

"The same goes for jobs. You must pretend things are fine, even if they are not. I know it's not fair, but it's not just models who are judged on their appearance, so much of life is about giving off the impression you know what you're doing."

Kevin chuckled as he leaned down. "I guess if people get the impression that you're barely holding it together they won't have much faith in you."

Alison giggled as she looked down. "Sadly, it does not help. I'll see if I can get that video taken down, though I don't think Chandler's going to do what I ask after tonight. And, to be fair, you did come off a tad rushed at times to everyone."

"Well, I can't deny I let my anxiety get the better of me at times. I can blame family genes, but I know it's me not having the willpower to fight it back. It's—it's just hard at times, you know? Things are so fast paced that there hardly seems to be any time to say much of anything. Then a lot of time I'm so anxious to say what I want to say before time runs out that I just make it worse.

"It just feels like people don't have time to get anything across these days. Sorry for rambling, it's my fault for not being able to make my point faster and clearer, that's cost me a lot."

"Even back when we were in school together you would take a while to get to your answers. But trust me, I get it. To be honest, half the time it's exhausting to me, like I'm hanging on to one crazy ride that I can barely hold on to. You know, it's been forever since I just hung out. When I spent the night with Teri at her place, it was nearly like learning how to bike again, just casually hanging out.

"Me and the other models are so busy with work that when the job ends its just preparing for the next one. It's like an endless race where we only have time to catch our breath. Even if we share a room on a job, we are all too busy planning for the next gig to socialize most of the time. Honestly, it would be nice to just take it easy for a bit. So, how about it, Kevin? Want to hang out?"

"Huh? What do you mean?"

Alison winked as she looked up. "I mean, just hang out at Teri's house so we can talk and all that? You know, like how friends do?"

Kevin saw Alison was sincere, and he asked. "You mean, alone? Is that okay?"

"Why, is that not okay with you? Kevin, I want to try the whole hanging out with friends thing again, like the old days. But I'm counting on you to be mature about it. I trust you, and when I think about it, I only have a handful of people I can trust, so let me down and you're going to pay, got it?"

Kevin saw Alison's response was playful before he said. "Don't worry Alison, I never want to do anything that would make you unhappy."

"I know, if I didn't see that, I would not invite you. C'mon, let me tell Teri and the others."

"Sure Alison, whatever you need."

Alison helped Kevin up before the two went back inside. In short order, Alison went in the back to see Cammy and Carlos talking. "Hey guys, how's it looking? Hope Chandler did not explode on anyone."

"No worries Ali, seems his dad is not done exploding on him," Carlos retorted dryly. "Chandler looked so freaked out he went into the bathroom. Won't be pretty when he does come out."

"Sounds like it. Guys, I've had enough drama for one night. I know it's not even seven yet, but mind if I head back? I just need some quiet time."

"Sure, you earned it, girl. And Alison, don't worry. No matter what happens, things will be okay. No matter what Chandler tried to pull, we know you were not part of it."

"Carlos, thanks. I just need a bit of time to rethink what I want my life to be about."

Cammy was about to respond when she noticed Kevin was in the back before she raised an eyebrow. "And he's a part of that process? What are you doing, Ali?"

"Be nice, Cammy. I just want to catch up with a friend of mine before things are done here, that's all. I care about him enough to do that much."

Cammy saw Alison did not seem to have any hesitation before she moaned. "If you want to play around, then that's your problem. Just don't do anything that will cause problems for Starlight, looks like we have enough crap hitting the fan as it is."

"Relax Cammy, this is not about work, it's just for me."

With a wave, Alison left them before Chandler could see her and led Kevin back down.

As Carlos saw Alison go, he was about to say something, but he saw Chandler burst out of the bathroom door. Carlos saw that he looked like he was in a daze. Everyone was quiet as Chandler asked. "Was, that Alison who just went out?"

"Not sure dude," Carlos casually said. "But any gal would be in a hurry to leave seeing a dude who looks like he's about to snap. What the hell happened?"

Chandler winced as he looked down. "Father, he misunderstands everything. Damn it, why did Alison have to be so impulsive? Is she still here?"

"Forget it, kid," Bright threw in casually as he finished his drink. "One way or another, that girl's gone as far as you're concerned. Might as well aim on what you can salvage, mate."

Chandler eyed Bright for a few moments before he yelled out in frustration. "Goddamn it, maybe Alison was just too poorly raised to see things clearly. Even so, I'll not leave tonight empty handed. It's too late to change things now, this pathetic town's fate is sealed."

"Sorry, whose town are you calling pathetic, son?"

Chandler winced as he saw Mayor Martin walk in, looking anything but amused. Springfield's leader cleared his throat before he walked up. "Sorry you're not having a good night, but to be honest I'm not having much of a good night either when I'm being told you're lying about just how this sponsorship was going to work. Now, I knew we would have to pay back anyone that would have donated money to get us back on our feet, but that's a far cry from just outright trying to annex this town like your company's Russia or China or something!"

"Like a small-town hack like you even knows how business is really conducted. If you did, you would not be at this state, mate! Everything was window dressing to make it seem better than it is, but when it comes down to it, you're too weak to survive without being put under new management, so you should be grateful some of you will get to be brought into the new era and not be left behind like the rest of the losers."

"Maybe that's how you see things, but my town has enough pride to not just roll over. You're getting ahead of yourself son, we never formally agreed to anything and now I'm not feeling much motivated to seal the deal."

"Mayor…don't let base emotions be your undoing. A town like this is doomed, so you either take what you can get, or you will drag things out a few more years till you have no say in the matter at how this town will change."

"Maybe…but at least it will be our choice to the very end. So, for now, if you can kindly get the hell out of my sight, I would be very appreciative."

Chandler saw how angry the mayor and just about everyone else around him looked before his eye twitched and he noticed Cammy.

She was finishing her drink as he looked in her direction. Chandler walked over to her. "You know, Cammy… I realize you and I have more in common than I previously…"

Before he could even finish, Cammy slapped him so hard he fell down. As many around her laughed, the blond woman gave Chandler the evil eye. "Don't even start, Chandler. I'm no one's sloppy seconds. You're crazy if you think I would want to be anywhere near the toxic situation you're now in. Get over yourself."

As Chandler cursed incoherently, Sam chuckled. "Well, clear as day that all the money in the world can't buy class, huh Bright?"

"You said it, Sam."

The two clinked their drinks together before going back to talk with Carlos about a few things, as everyone tried to avoid Chandler.

12

Reaching the Intertwined
Path of Shared Dreams

eanwhile, a person with a bit more class managed to find her friend after asking around. Alison saw Teri and Bart were still chatting casually right outside the parking lot. Upon seeing Alison, Teri raised an eyebrow. "There you are, girl! What's been going on? Heard there was a fight? The guy Bart punched Chandler and people are saying all sort of things!"

Bart saw Kevin looking at him before he shrugged. "Don't look at me, I just punched a jackass for being a jackass. Still, glad you're looking better dude. The way that prick was talking sounds like he ripped your heart out or something."

Kevin chuckled tensely as he said. "Well, things seemed rather bad for a while, but after the moment ended, I realized things were not quite as bad as I thought, thanks to Alison."

Alison saw Bart was looking at her intently before she cleared her throat. "A lot of people made mistakes; I just did not want things to get out of hand. Teri, is it okay if I go back to your place to hang out with Kevin? It's just been a while since we could talk alone in a more casual setting."

Teri raised an eyebrow as she leaned closer. "You sure you want to hang out one on one, Ali?"

"Don't worry, it will be fine. If worse comes to worse, I know where the pepper spray is. Your parents are going to be away till Monday, right?"

"Yeah, don't worry, no one to interrupt. Della wanted to catch up anyway and she has a spare bed. Just keep your eyes open."

"Of course. Thanks Teri."

Kevin saw his own friend smirk and he cleared his throat and went up to Bart. "Bart, so you punched Chandler for me? Thanks for having my back."

"What, you doubted me, bro? The jackass was just begging to be humbled. Helped that he pissed just about everyone else off, so I knew the crowd had my back."

"It's good to know that you're not alone. Hey Bart, sorry to leave you hanging but going to hang out with Alison for the rest of the night. You able to get an Uber back?"

"And waste cash with that? Hell no, you take the Uber back man, it's on your account anyway."

"What? But...but it could be late."

"And Uber drivers are around all night, dude. What, afraid of getting picked up by Jigsaw?"

Kevin sighed and he gave Alison a sheepish grin. Alison shrugged as she stated. "Just behave or you will find yourself falling out of the car before you can blink." Bart flashed another half-lopped smile before he punched Kevin in the arm. "You will thank me later bro, trust me. Did not want to get your hopes up, but this pal of yours might be more on the level than first thought. Just read the room, okay?"

"I got it Bart, thanks."

The two friends pounded fists before Kevin looked at Alison. She saw Kevin hand over his keys before she said. "Just be careful with my seat, okay? Got a lot of memos and stuff around the car."

"Oh, of course just let me know when it's okay." Alison giggled before leading Kevin to her car. He saw Alison blush a bit before they got up to her blue vehicle.

He peeked inside her window and saw there were magazines and other things all over the seats. He raised an eyebrow before Alison looked flustered. "It looks sloppy, but it's not just random stuff. I just have to have a lot of things at times to prepare for and I need a lot of stuff open at once."

"Don't worry about it. It's still a lot neater than some of my other friends' cars. Just glad it's full of magazines and not just food."

Alison giggled a bit as she unlocked the door. "Thanks. The ride should only take ten minutes."

"All right. I'll just let my folks know I might not be back till tomorrow."

"Go for it."

The two got in the car, and as Alison saw Kevin looking like he was using all of his willpower to not look too excited after he was done with his call, she asked, "Kevin don't mean to put you on the spot, but I have to know. Am I *really* the only woman you thought about your entire life?"

"What? I mean, of course not," Kevin answered nervously. "I mean, there were girls I liked in college and after that. It just didn't work out. I mean, I liked them, but they just did not like me back in that way. Some already had boyfriends, some just had no interest in me whatsoever. Ahm...sorry, I know its rude to talk to a woman about other women and all that."

Alison saw Kevin's shamed look and then she smiled. "It's okay. I'm just glad you were not thinking about me the entire time and all. Don't worry, you can talk to me about it. I want to know what you've been through."

Kevin saw Alison was sincere, so he smiled and said, "Thanks."

As Alison drove to Teri's house, Kevin talked about the girls he liked over the years. While Kevin was worried by the end of it, Alison would drop him at another house and drive off, aside from a few giggles she did not mock Kevin but just gave short responses.

It was the first time in years anyone listened to him about what he went through, and before Kevin knew it, they were at Teri's house. As Alison turned off the car, she took a deep breath before she said. "Well Kevin, I am glad you did not turn into one of those crazy women-hating nutjobs that just rage on the internet all day, after being turned down so many times.

"As long as you're telling me the truth, sounds like aside from the few awkward one-liners you been saying since before I left, you didn't do anything too bad. From what you told me, sounds like in the end it's just that well…frankly just that even if they did not have anything against you, they did not find you interesting enough to want to go to the next step.

"Many of them seemed to just prefer to ghost you to avoid making things awkward. I admit, I've done it a few times in the past myself with a few guys who were just a little *too* excited to hear from me."

Kevin nodded slowly as he got out of the car. "I don't think I was being too aggressive, but if things went as I thought they should have gone, well, things would have been a lot different. To be honest, when social media started, the rules were not really clear to me about what was okay, or maybe I'm just trying to beat around the bush that I made bad judgment calls. I posted too many things on someone's Facebook page to try and look supportive, only for her to suddenly vanish.

"I never meant to be harmful or anything, I just wanted to show I supported what they cared about. But after being shown the context of a situation or two, I could understand how it might come across differently on the other side. I know now that I have more problems than most."

Alison saw Kevin was looking ashamed again, "You're flawed Kevin, but *everyone's* flawed. I sure as hell am. Guess it's a good thing we were not talking online for years before we met again. To be fair, I made my own online mistakes, let's just say, they were a bit different than what you might have made, but ones I wish I could take back all the same. Why else would I let some smooth-talking two-faced "Aussie Boy" asshole string me along for years? It was a nice ride, but I did keep my eyes down to keep myself from thinking how it was going to end."

"Sorry, I really hope I did not mess up everything you had going on Alison."

"Don't worry, you did not ruin anything, Kevin. I found out that Chandler had gotten me a movie role. But it was a role as a stripper where I was cast for my body over anything I would say or do."

Kevin looked shocked before he paused. "Wait, that's bad, right? Sorry, I don't want to be judgmental about your choices. Whatever works for you, if that's what you want. Well, unless you're killing people, but I don't think we are talking about that. Sorry, there's a lot of ways this can lead to a wrong answer."

Alison giggled as she leaned back. "Thanks for being considerate. I'm not that prudish of a person, but it depends on how it comes across. I don't like feeling like I'm just a meat bag, or wall decoration. It's true that when the world nearly stood still, I made online videos and made use of my sexuality to get attention, but I always tried to make it be about something aside from just eye candy, something more. You know, I started out just wanting to take photos? But no one noticed, at least, not enough to live off. So, to get attention, I started making silly poses in the photos, and it got attention despite how silly I felt.

"Then when everyone was more or less trapped for so long, by chance Chandler noticed my photos, and with his help we were able to make online videos that looked like I was going places using the most recent tech. People were yearning to feel like they were somewhere, so my videos let them forget how reality was. At least then, I was feeling like I was doing more than just being eye candy. With this last stunt though, I was clearly just the decoration for Chandler's stage.

"Chandler said it was a stepping-stone to greater things, but it also seemed like he was doing a deal for a buddy for a business deal as some power play. But in the end, even if he was conning himself, he was *using* me as a pawn. Even if I'm an important piece, I'm not just a ladder for someone else to climb higher."

Kevin clenched his fist tightly as he looked down. "Well, I knew Chandler a lot less than you, Alison. But he did seem like a guy who saw people how he wanted to see them."

"He is like that a lot, a lot more than I wanted to admit. He is a damn good salesman in many ways. And I'd be lying if I said he didn't know how to make things fun. I guess he knew how to make things good enough to forget about the rest of the world, even my dad."

Kevin looked conflicted as he said, "I didn't bring it up because, honestly, I did not want to rock the boat, but what *did* happen with your dad? I just remember before you left, you said your parents were arguing a lot, and then you left. You know, some of your friends said it was to get away from me. I mostly blocked it out."

Alison saw Kevin looked distraught before she squeezed his hand warmly. "I hope they were just lashing out because they were sad too, because that's not the reason. My mom had to get far away from dad, that's all it was. My dad cheated on my mom with a younger woman.

"Call it the cliché daddy issues, but it was devastating seeing him leave for another woman. Despite his excuses, it came down to 'I enjoyed being with her more than you and mom.' It kind of leaves a mental scar.

"It was worse that in spite of all that, my mom left me with him because she did not feel like she could handle raising me on her own and it made me feel neglected. I guess I've been drawn to Chandler and guys like him who make me feel special.

"In high school it nearly cost me big, but I was lucky someone was around to bail me out of my own mistakes. I thought I was smarter by the time I met Chandler. But needless to say, I'm having second thoughts. From the start he knew how to make me happy, or at least, to keep me entertained. But I realized he wanted to keep me entertained enough so that I did not ask questions. Still, I guess I have not really stopped to think for years. Things are, simpler that way, I guess."

Kevin thought for a few moments before chuckling. "It makes sense in a way. For years I had too much time to over think things and I guess it has not made things better."

"Everything is better with moderation, Kevin. For a long time, I just thought about what would help me get the job, and then what would help me advance my job. But I've been working so hard that I realized I'm not even sure what I'm working for anymore.

"I have an apartment, but I think I have more things in my car than I do there. I just don't have time to waste with home stuff. But I wonder if I'm just rushing so much to not have to think of what I missed?"

Kevin saw Alison look troubled before he asked. "I mean, far as I can tell it's not just you, Alison. Lots of people I know these days hardly have time to live. I think society just demands so much of us that we must spend so much time just to hang on that we forget there is more to life than that. But hey, if you enjoy the ride then that's something, right? After all, home's where the heart is and all that?"

Alison let out another giggle as she looked at Teri's door. "True enough. Well, I try and make wherever I stay more than a day feel like home. And thankfully Teri and her parents are rather proud of their home here. Want a tour of my home away from home?"

Kevin saw Alison's mock curtsy before he grinned and bowed back. "I'd be honored to."

As Kevin proceeded, Alison flicked off her shoes before she undid her ponytail. "So, did you have time to eat before? I mean, I think we have a few pieces of pizza left from lunch yesterday. I admit, the Pacinos still know their pizza. Good thing too, they are one of the few pizza places still open at this point around here."

"All the more impressive since they got bought out twice. Some traditions live on if they are stubborn enough. So, just curious, Alison. After all the places you've been, it's not been that lame coming back to Springfield, has it?"

She paused as she looked at a few pictures before she smiled. "Oh well, it's obviously not Paris or Rome or anything. Coming back after all this time has made the flaws rather clear, but also its strengths. It is nice to be able to relax for a change."

Kevin saw Alison's tranquil look before he shrugged. "It is nice not being cramped. Honestly, it gets a tad isolating at times. At this point, it's hard to find people to just hang out with. True, the city's not too far, but it's expensive just to go there to chat about stuff you know? But cheaper than living in the city, I guess."

"Oh…trust me, just being in the city does not make it easier to hang out. These days, with how demanding things are, even when someone's living in the same room you hardly see them. It's just how it is to make ends meet these days.

"Sometimes it's for the best. Honestly, my roommate and I are having issues now. Well, mostly me having issues with her not picking up after herself and not respecting having the TV on too loud."

"Oh, you too, huh? I had a roommate like that in college that got rather messy. He never showered and kept me up all night watching game shows."

"Oh my god, that sounds insane."

"And that was *before* he put glass shards on my bed after one messed up drinking session. Well, it's a long story but we have time, right?"

After an amused nod, Kevin went on to talk about his experiences in college, before Alison did the same. Hours flew by as the two talked about everything from friends to trips they were on, and Kevin found the two were able to talk as easily as when they were still in school together.

After laughing about Alison talking about her fashion shoot in Paris, Kevin eyed the clock. Alison noticed this before she raised an eyebrow. "What's wrong Kevin, bored already?"

"Not at all Alison. It's the opposite, just wish that a full moon brought extra hours with it, so it did not have to end, and things have to go back to the routine."

"Oh, come now Kevin, not like you're going back to prison, right?"

"True, I mean, if the thing with Carlos worked out, maybe I'll get a chance to move to where I should be in life? Though based on what happened with Chandler, guess I should not bet on it."

"Not as much as you might think, Kevin. Carlos *was* impressed and wants to help. But it's just that well, honestly, we don't have much room for many full-time spots these days."

"Sadly, I've heard that so many times that it's my default assumption of what I'm going to hear at this point. Well, just hope that video won't make it even harder to get somewhere."

"Don't worry, Kevin, embarrassing stuff from the internet does not stick too long as long as it's nothing *really* bad. Unless they are already prudes, most people know anyone can be caught on camera when they are not ready for it. Just got to not let it define you, ok? After all, that's not what you want to be known as, right?"

"You're right, Alison."

"Thought so. Just hang in there. I did see your trips and some of the stuff you did. I know it does not feel like it at times, but you have done some stuff that I have not seen anyone do, even guys like Chandler. You just have to feel proud about the stuff you do, and people will notice more."

"That makes sense. I guess it's a vicious cycle, you know?"

"I know, but I think you're somebody Kevin, so remember that. Think of it this way, Kevin, at least you don't have to go back to be grilled by your boss's boss."

He winced as he looked down. "Er, sorry about that. I really hope your job's not in trouble because of me, Alison. I mean, you said Chandler helped get you your job, right? Damn it, I wish I could do something but well, the options I think I have might just make things worse for you."

"It's okay, Kevin, I'll manage. His dad may be part of Starlight, but thankfully not the *only* part. I think I made it clear I was not part of Chandler's plan, so if things blow up for him, I won't go down with the ship. Thankfully Carlos and enough of the others like me enough to stick up for me.

"Though, to be honest, I'm not too sure how long this will be how my life is. Starlight's fine enough, but I know I can't be a model forever. I don't want to be one of those women who are only fooling themselves."

"That's fine Alison, you do what you want to do, of course. It's just, what's the dream you want your life to be? I guess it's more than

194

dressing up as a humanoid bird?"

Alison giggled again as she thought back to her last outfit for the gig. "Not quite. I don't mind dressing up in kooky outfits, but *only* if stands for something. Maybe it sounds naïve, but I did see modelling as an artist, to make statements about things.

"I was never naïve enough to think I would have to do stuff I did not like to make ends meet and get ahead, but it's just that I hoped the stuff I did mattered and was more than just being wall paper, more than just fluff, something that mattered, you know what I mean? But maybe that's just silly excuses a girl makes to push herself."

Kevin saw Alison looked conflicted, and he got up and sat next to her. "We all want to hope what we do matters, Alison. The stuff I do for Bright, the book I hope to get published, I hope all of it proves I was a somebody and all that.

"I mean, I'm not going to pretend I'm an expert on fashion or modelling or most of that stuff, Alison, but Carlos and the others did seem impressed with what you were doing. So even if Chandler was leading you along, it won't take too long to rise up, right?"

"Yeah, but rise up into what? The number one wallpaper that is up front until you're used up and thrown away? Like, for all the talk about embodying the future, in the end Chandler was just pushing me to dress up for the future he and the people he was plotting with to look like. I'm not a damn company mascot. I don't think that last gig really symbolized the past, the present, or the future of Springfield in the end."

Kevin paused for a minute before he raised an eyebrow. "Well...not sure if it's a good idea but I had an idea. You remember that tree you use to like a lot? Old Snappy? Well, it's been cut down since you were gone but they planted a new tree recently. I mean, it's hardly more than a few buds but it still is like, symbolic of the past and the future of the town hand in hand. I don't know, sounds right in my head but I know that's not the word on what makes good art."

Alison saw Kevin looked excited for a moment, before looking anxious. But his look caused her to flash a hopeful smile as she leaned up to him. "Honestly, that sounds lovely. Do they have any photos of how it looks like now?"

"Sure. Hell, I even covered the new tree's planting. I mean, I like to try and cover this stuff, so that the channel is more than just promoting one local sports thing or town budget thing. One second."

Kevin went on his phone and in a bit got a few pictures up. Alison looked at the pictures, and while he was anxious for a few moments he felt a surge of relief as Alison smiled. "This is great Kevin! I remember they said that the tree was cut down, not enough time to even hear they planted a new one. Well, a new tree does not sound very stylish, unless one can make a spin on it. It might not fit the plan Starlight had, but it's something I would like to do."

"Glad I could show it to you, Alison. Just sorry it's just as you guys are about to go. Guess even guys as pro as Starlight can't whip up a gig in less than a day."

Alison paused before she looked at the direction of the house that went to Teri's house's basement. After blinking a few times, she blushed. "Well, not a full performance, no, but if things come together fast, it's possible for something to be put together, maybe even something magical.

"Kevin…a true model does not need to have stylish outfits precisely spat out for every occasion to make a work of art if they are bold enough.

"Like, I've done a *few* shoots with body paint. It can be a bit risqué, but if it gets the point across, I don't mind giving a risqué shoot if it gives the right message across."

Kevin cleared his throat as he looked around. "Oh, have you? I mean, I'll take your word for it and all."

Alison saw Kevin looked uneasy before she leaned back. "Kevin, you can be honest with me. Did you see my Instagram profile?"

"I mean, I may have seen a few things, but I swear I was just seeing, um, all that you were up to."

"It's okay, Kevin, if I made it so you did not need to do anything special to access it that means I knew anyone could see it. It was a rough day when my mom saw it. Sometimes…I wonder if seeing that I was doing stuff like that pushed her over the edge health wise. I don't know, she got too ill to talk to after that time. But, while there are some things I wish I did better, I don't regret doing what I needed to do in order to keep going forward.

"Like what I said before, I'm willing to push what some would see as boundaries, if it's in the right environment, I'm willing to make a scene.

"Just must make sure the conditions are right. And so, about that Kevin, I'm sure you know about wood fairies, right? I know you're not in your element, but you think you could handle a photo op?"

"What, seriously? You mean, with you?"

"What, you think Cammy's up for a photo at the moment? I can't do it myself. Lucky for you, selfie sticks can't work well covering the back or you would be out of luck. Still…this *does* require someone who can work professionally."

"Why…is it hard to put the outfit together?"

"It's rather basic, it's just, well, it's what you put it on. All right, here it goes. Kevin, I'm about to take a major risk on the assumption that I can trust you, okay? This outfit is just body paint that Teri's mom has here for her own art projects in the basement. The only thing that makes it tricky is that well, it's body paint, as in my body. And well, since I don't want to half ass it, then that means, it will be a *full* body paint."

Kevin blinked a few times before his eyes widened in shock. He gulped before stepping back. "Wait, Alison, are you saying what I think you're saying? Just wanted to be clear, wanted to make sure this is not a test or something."

Alison just laughed as she leaned back and unbuttoned the first button of her blouse. "It is a test, Kevin. I want to see if you can behave professionally. So, can you still keep your cool even after I show you all I got?"

"I mean, I…I don't know how to answer that."

"At least you're honest about it. Well…guess we will have to see how much control you have in the moment of truth. So, unless you have any objections, I'll get undressed now and we can get started."

"Wait Alison. I might regret this for the rest of my life, but if this is you acting drunk or something, are you sure you want to go through with this? I just don't want one good moment only for everything to be ruined the next day."

Alison paused for a moment, and then just laughed out loud. "Oh Kevin, I promise you I'm not drunk. I'm glad you think that way, truly. I know this might not be the most normal thing for friends to do when they hang out. But the truth is that if I can get naked in front of strangers for shoots, I can do it in front of someone I trust. I would normally be worried that I would give someone the wrong impression, but well, the truth is you're already crazy about me, right?"

Kevin paused before his jaw dropped. As he stuttered to say something, Alison giggled again as she got up to pat him on the shoulder. "It's okay Kevin, you don't have to make excuses. So, if you're already going to think about me, might as well think of my body properly and not a distorted version, right? Still, promise you won't take any pictures of me other than the ones for my project?"

Kevin quickly tried to retain his composure as he nodded. "Oh, of course Alison. Scout's honor. I mean it's not like I've never seen a woman's body before, no need to jeopardize a friendship over that."

"So, you *have* been in front of a naked woman before?"

"Well, there was this one beach on that one vacation, from a distance. But I, well, it was not someone I knew, up this close and all."

"Is that right? Well, I'll guide you on how you should be reacting, okay?"

"Of course."

Alison winked as she unbuttoned her blouse, and quickly shrugged it off and put it on the chair behind her. Kevin tried to keep cool saying he saw her in some revealing outfits during previous shoots in the gig, but it took more of his focus as she unzipped her jeans and quickly tugged them down.

Alison went for her bra and saw Kevin looking stressed before she smirked. "I'll allow you a few moments to take in the view, but if you start to drool the plan's canceled, got it?"

"Of course. You're my friend, not some doll."

"Sure, you say that now, but can you say that even after this?"

With a wink Kevin saw Alison unhook her bra and casually fling it on the chair. Kevin tried not to look too excited as he saw Alison's newly exposed chest settle into place before he just kept his face stoic to not come off as boorish.

Alison saw Kevin look as still as a statue and giggled again before causally pulling the last piece of clothing off her hips. Alison saw Kevin widen his eyes before she put her arms on her hips. "So, be honest with me Kevin, does it live up to the hype?"

Kevin took a deep breath before he nodded. "Alison, it's far beyond anything I dreamed of. I can see, you do take care of yourself very well."

Alison went right up to Kevin's face, and wrinkled her nose in amusement. "Well of course, can't try and be a pro if you slack off, right? All right, so ready to go to work? You think you can draw this on my back?"

Alison got her phone again and got the picture she wanted before she put it in front of Kevin's face. After making sure his eyes were on the picture, she smirked. It's nothing too complicated, but can't really put it on my own back."

"Just that? Yah sure, I drew symbols like that all the time in art class for some of my projects…though they were a bit smaller. Hell, it even reminds me of…"

"Of Mystique from X-men right?"

"You saw that too?"

"Well duh, I mean learning about the process for an outfit is a no duh thing for anyone in our biz. Plus, she, Psylocke and a few of the others looked rather bad ass."

"No arguments there, even if the last film ruined a lot of them. So, is there anything else we need to go through, or should we just start this?"

"Just get me a garbage bag or two so we don't get paint all over the floor, okay?"

Kevin nodded and quickly got some garbage bags as Alison got the paint ready. As she started to paint herself, she saw Kevin had the bags spread out already before she said. "So, you think you can paint the town mascot on? I'll try and not flinch, just don't get shaky hands."

"Got it."

With a look of trust between the two, Kevin begun to paint the outline of a cat's face. With only limited space it was no masterpiece, but as Alison glanced at the mirror, she was content with what she saw. It took some focus, but Kevin was determined to prove to Alison he could be professional and got everything done, despite the very unusual circumstances.

It took a few drinks and snacks to get through, but before they knew it, the process was complete. Alison realized there was no more places to paint and looked at herself. She saw how her green and pink body looked and glanced at her back before she said to Kevin. "Well, might not be as good looking as something from a movie, but I say since we just put this together on a whim, it looks rather damn good."

Kevin saw how relieved Alison looked before he grinned widely.

"Glad you like how it came out. Wanted to make sure it came out as you wanted it to."

"I know it's been a long night Kevin, but it's not over yet. Unless we see this through, we did all this for nothing."

"Oh right, of course. So, how do you want to pull this off? I mean, as stylish as you may look now, still might cause a scene if we are seen. Hell, kind of might get arrested."

"I'll wear a jacket to not bring attention. There is still more than one way to get into Old Snappy, right?"

"Yeah, it's mostly the same. Long as we watch ourselves, should be able to make it to Old Snappy without being seen. Been a long night, but just want it to end well."

"Don't worry, with the time it is now we can pass it off as an early morning jog if a cop or someone else sees us along the way. No matter what, Kevin, I promise this won't end badly, trust me."

Kevin saw Alison looked determined before he said. "I do, and no matter how it ends I'll make sure you get a good shot. Just, if like there are coyotes or drunks it might take a while to work it out."

"Oh, come on Kevin, don't need to make things up just to be dramatic."

"Oh. . . I'm not making up the coyotes...they've been all over the place since you left. One killed my neighbor's cat a few years ago, that really sucked. But don't worry, this is not the time of year they should be around. Well, we'll see, right?"

Kevin cleaned up as Alison got a raincoat and the other things she needed. After a final recap, the two got back in the car. Alison wore a town sports cap so her face paint would not be noticed too much and the duo took off.

Despite them being up most of the night, at this point the two were both excited enough to keep going. They got to the side of the local park easily enough, and the place where they parked had a hill to prevent people on the road from seeing the car.

The two had to duck a few times when they heard a car, and there were one or two moments that they were sure they saw eyes in the trees, but after a few minutes of laying low, they managed to get to the remains of Old Snappy and the new tree planted in front of it.

As Alison looked at its current state she smirked at Kevin. "Great, it's as good as we are going to get. Let's get it done while the sun is in the right position. Go from the back just in case anyone comes this way. Ready Kevin?"

He saw an eager look in her eye before he nodded. "Yup. Just let me know if you want any changes."

Alison smiled before handing Kevin her phone for the photos. After checking the stump to make sure there was nothing sharp for her to stand on, she discarded everything and stood on the stump. She glanced at Kevin getting into position before she smirked. "Make sure to get my good side, okay?"

Kevin saw Alison crouching down, looking like she was a mystical feline creature ready to go on the prowl and took a picture from her side to get her face without making the shot seem too raunchy. After taking a few more shots he turned to the front, where Alison gave off elegant beckoning poses, like a deity commanding a forest to rise at her will.

After a few more shots, Kevin just nodded. Alison flicked her hair back and jumped down before putting her hand out for the phone. She saw the pictures Kevin took, and smiled in approval. "These are pretty damn good, Kevin! For not having the best lenses, you moved into just the right place."

"Oh well, I have had some practice at covering you all during your gig, and I have spent more than a few years getting grilled by Bright, Sam, and the others on what's the best angle for a photo, though this is the most fun I've had, without a doubt. So, is this what you wanted? It's really okay for you to just post this as part of the same stuff you have been doing in town?"

"Not going to make this part of the gig, Kevin. This will be part of my personal creations on my own stuff. Might not fit a homely photo op for the kids, but fits more for the whole symbolizing the embracing my roots to be a force of nature. In some ways that's true."

"It's all about one's perspective, I guess. I just hope your audience will like the pics. Er...for the right reasons."

"Don't worry, I think they will. It's not going to change the world or anything, but it will remind people I can do more than fluff pieces, that I'm not passive but can take action in my own way.

"Thanks, Kevin, was a long-twisted road, but I needed a reminder of what I'm trying to do before I gave up."

"No problem Alison, glad I could really help you while you were here. Glad I can make at least some positive differences."

Alison saw Kevin looked conflicted before she paused and got in front of him. "It does not have to be, Kevin. I have an idea. All of this has gotten me to want to take a break from the gigs. I think I want to do my own thing, to make my own story.

"More or less, I want to take time off to go across the country and make my own shots, just for my personal brand. I *could* use a camera man, so how would you like to be my partner for the gig?"

Kevin blinked a few times to make sure he heard things before he looked at her. "Wait, seriously? I mean, don't get me wrong, I'm just happy you would want to work more with me, but you sure you want me instead of one of your professional co-workers?"

Alison just giggled as she leaned back. "It's harder to get Starlight members to do side projects than you might think with contract obligations and all that. I mean, I had one who could have done it, but he and Chandler were close friends and that might not have been a good idea.

"It's legit easier to get a part-time spot than switch a full-time employee from an assignment. Sorry to say that means there won't be any health care or any other full-time perks, but it will be more than what you're making at the moment."

"That's not a high bar to pass, but I'll take it anyway. Alison, this is better than I ever dared hope. Thanks so much."

"Don't thank me yet, partner. You know not *every* shot is going to be as risque as this one, right? Just to be clear, I trust you enough for this, but we are not suddenly girlfriend and boyfriend. For the sake of not making things too messy, it would be best if we both got separate rooms. Do...you understand?"

Kevin chuckled as he leaned back. "Well, reaching too far for the stars seems like a good way to get burned, and if this is what makes you feel safe, then that's how it goes. But I mean, we can still chill when you're up for it, right?"

"If I'm not too tired. If it's a good day, I might even be up for a round or two of Mario Kart if that's still something you like."

"Well, if you're still up for that, then sure as hell sounds good to me. If you're up for it I even have a few new games you might like."

"Just as long as you make things easy for a casual gamer. I mostly just like to blow off steam. Kevin, I know you're excited, but you do realize I'm talking about driving across the country, right? Unless I'm missing something, you told me before you hardly drove out of town?"

Kevin hesitated for a moment before he told her, "It's true, this might be biting off more than I can chew. But I've been saying for years if I just got a chance, I could turn things around. And, if I back down now, I'd be a hypocrite, so I don't want to be like that."

"Oh Kevin, is that just because you want to be with me?"

"I mean, can't it be a little of both? I mean, maybe I would do this for anyone, but I would need to trust them first. And well…I already trust you. No matter what, I know this is something I want to do. Just, let me know what the plan is, and I'll be there."

Alison looked touched as she grasped his hand. "Oh Kevin." The two locked eyes and were quiet for a moment. Kevin did not even breathe as Alison got closer. For a moment it looked like they were going to kiss, till suddenly Alison yawned.

She stepped back before she giggled. "Well, before anything, I think we better get back to Teri's place. As revved up as going through with this made me, it's starting to set in that its almost morning and I have not slept. Better plan out the details when we can think straight, ok?"

Despite not getting quite the reaction he was hoping for, Kevin could not help but laugh. "Yeah, passing out here might make things a drag. All right, sleep first, planning the future later. Ready to head back then?"

Kevin held out his hand to Alison, and she did not hesitate to take it as she gave a sweet smile, before the two went off to figure out how to plan out the future.

Epilogue

Life's Tango

Kevin and Alison got to Teri's place just before passing out. Kevin woke up to his cell phone ringing, while Alison woke up to Teri entering her room. After Alison calmly explained why she was dressed how she was, she went to talk to Carlos and a few of his superiors about her new plan, while Kevin talked to his parents.

It took a bit of negotiating on Alison's side, and Kevin had to weather nearly an hour of his dad's ranting before he got it through his father's head that this was both legit and something he wanted to do. With some nudging from his mother, Kevin's father relented.

While it was not instantaneous, Kevin and Alison, with some help from Carlos and a few of Alison's friends, were able to work out a timetable. Before he knew it, he was packing things into his car and getting ready to go with Alison on a trip across the nation that would take months.

At the moment, Kevin was in the process of packing his trunk and was about to slam it when Bart caught it. As Kevin looked shocked his friend chuckled. "Forgetting something, dude?"

"Um…I think I got everything Bart. Why, did something fall out?"

"Nah, but it's something that should be in there. Need a wrench in case you get a flat, dude. If you're going to pull this off, you're going to need it in case you get a flat or something."

"Thanks, Bart. Alright this is everything now, I...Augh!"

Kevin slammed the car door so fast that it slammed back open and hit him in the face.

For a moment all Kevin saw was white, like he was suddenly in a white room before he shook his head. He staggered a bit and saw an ambulance at the end of the block with its driver just looking out the vehicle before he chuckled dryly. "Man, I know they keep improving technology, but they are jumping the gun just a bit."

Bart looked back before he sighed, then shrugged. "C'mon dude, don't be like that. Someone's always in trouble some place in the world, but we just got to focus on moving forward as much as we can, right? Don't get psyched out and fall right before moving on, okay?"

As Kevin's vision returned, he chuckled anxiously. "Well, would suck if this trip ended before it even begun. Talk about jumpy. . . just wanted to make sure I have everything. Guess this is going to be a bit longer than my usual rides."

"That's putting it lightly, dude. I mean let's be real for a moment. You were stressed out going to the next county to try out that one restaurant I wanted to try, and here you are about to go all off over the country for months?"

"I mean, that's true. I guess there is just too much motivating me for me to back down now."

"You're really going to head off on a road trip that's only thinly planned out to chase tail, huh? You sure she's not going to bail as soon as a bump in the road comes along?"

"I mean, I can't see the future, man. But I trust her enough to try this. I mean, here she is now."

Bart turned around and saw that Alison's car was indeed in the process of parking before he snickered. "Well, always good when a girl sticks to her word."

Kevin saw Alison walk out of the car and smiled. Alison smiled back as she saw Kevin was nearly packed. "Hey Kevin! Glad to see you're ready to go, got a big day today! Oh, hey Bart, glad you're doing well."

"Same to you. Just curious, that mop-head of a former boyfriend still looking for me to get even?"

"Don't have to worry about that. Chandler's so worried about salvaging his standing with his father he already left the country."

"Not worried either way, but cool beans that karma catches up to a spoiled brat. Well, glad you woke up before you went down with the ship, Alison. Speaking of ships, you two really plotted your course? If not, it's going to derail really damn fast."

"Don't worry, Bart, we planned it so the meeting places are all easy enough to get to. Well that's how it supposed to be, but you can only take it one step at a time, right? You could say we are starting off in memory lane. To think it looks the same as before I left here."

Kevin looked at his apartment with shame as he rubbed the back of his head. "Yeah…sorry it's more or less the same sight it was all those years ago. I had ideas for how to change things…my dad would never go for it because it did not fit his vision."

Bart saw Kevin's embarrassment and snickered. "Not like you had the cash to pull off those changes yourself, right, dude?"

Alison saw Kevin's embarrassment and just smiled kindly at him. "Don't think about it too much, Kevin. My old house is not even around anymore. They just demolished it to make a McMansion that took up the whole block."

"Er…yeah. Don't feel too bad about it, Alison, it's not 'cause of your family, I think the people who moved in after you killed each other. It was messed up."

"Damn…seriously? Good thing we were not neighbors. Besides Kevin, it's not like nothing's changed around here. I can clearly see things are a bit grayer around here." Kevin paused before he heard a door open, and saw his parents come out. His mother looked happy to see Alison, while his father at least looked subdued. Kevin's mother smiled at once as she stepped forward. "Alison! It's so good to see you, dear."

"You too Mrs. Summers. Sorry you had to go through so much this past few years."

"It's okay dear, its nothing that will keep me down. I'm just glad I can retire knowing my son's on the path he needs to be. Glad you're able to figure out your own path as well dear."

"Thanks, it took a while, but I was able to get some clarity thanks to coming back here. I wish we could talk more, but we must stay on track to make sure we can make the appointment on time. It's going to be intense, but hopefully it's going to work out."

Kevin's father glanced at Alison carefully for a few moments before he cleared his throat. "Alison…just to be clear here, you're sure that if Kevin does this thing right it will help his career?"

Alison saw Biff trying not to show his anxiety before she took a deep breath and flicked some hair out of her eyes. "I can't promise it will give him a full-time job at the end of this. But it should help him get noticed by the right people. Stuff like this has helped a lot of my coworkers and friends get their careers to take off.

"And, since I know what worked for them, I'll be able to help Kevin make the right choices. Of course, he will have to carry his weight, but I promise I'll do what I can to make sure this helps him. He scratches my back and I'll scratch his, you know?"

Kevin saw his father looked amused at her playfulness before he chuckled. "Well, not like I did not take a risk when I was your age. Took a bit longer, but glad you found some initiative, boy. Guess you just needed the right c… never mind. But glad you're acting like a man and taking a leap, boy. No matter what happens, your old man will be proud of you. Just, remember to look where you leap, Kevin."

"I will dad, I will."

"Just…make sure you know what's going on before each stop okay, Kevin?" Kevin's mother muttered as she looked misty eyed. "And, no matter what, make sure to keep us in the loop. I knew things would be quieter after retiring, did not think it would be this quiet though."

Kevin saw his mother looking depressed and he hugged her. "Don't worry Mom, I'll make sure you're in the loop. Got to give you some fun stories for the day, right? Man, did not plan it like this, but with us and Bart leaving around the same time guess it's going to be quiet around here."

Bart laughed as he patted Kevin on the shoulder. "Guess your folks are going to have to relearn how to enjoy quality time. Well, I'll be having a blast setting things up in the home base. But hell, if you are able to stick to this and are where I am, give me a heads up and I'll be sure to meet yah for a drink. Might be a night call, but it's something."

"I'll make time bro, after all, moments with true friends are rare as hell, right?"

"Hell yeah. Sorry for being on your case from time to time. I know that someone who's hardly had any real major accomplishments in his life has little right to have pride. But it's just, you got to have *some* pride in myself you know?"

"It depends on what you're trying to be proud about. But you're not too much more out of touch than most people these days, so just got to keep your head out of the clouds, dude."

"Thanks man."

As the two-fist bumped, Bart saw Alison and flashed another half-lopped smile. 'Well, I ragged on you for years dude, but this time you seem to be doing more than just dreaming. You're doing what it takes to make it come true, so I'm down with that."

"Thanks Bart, I mean it. For how much I rag on you at times, hope you know how much it means to me that you still got my back after all of it."

"When we were all but roommates getting on each other's nerves it's bound to happen. But even though you can be a dumbass, at least you're a loyal one."

"Thanks…er…I think."

"Just don't get cocky kid, I know in some of the video games just when you're close to the goal you get too eager and blow it. Well, you're not going to get an extra life in this one bud."

"Trust me, I know, man. Well, that's why I'll touch base with you when I can to make sure I'm on track."

"I'm not your emergency line for your social life dude, boundaries, man! Besides, I might have some stuff of my own going on. Hell, might even follow up with Teri if she is on the level."

"As a matter of fact, Teri thought you were really fun, Bart. It's not as easy as it may have looked, so don't waste it."

"Noted Ali, thanks for being more on the level than I first figured. Just don't do a face turn now, those really piss me off."

"Don't worry, I'm not about to pull an Undertaker, that was really lame."

"Oh, you followed wrestling too? Cool beans."

"Well, it was mostly my dad, but it did leave an early impression on how style matters. Speaking of that, don't mean to rush you Kevin, but if we don't leave soon, might leave an early impression to the folks at Ratched Falls of being slackers."

"Well, that would be a sucky way to start off, right?" Kevin said wryly. Kevin saw his parents and Bart all laugh before he steeled himself. "Still, I have to admit Ratched Falls was not the kind of place I figured you would want to kick things off at, Alison."

"I know it's not what people think of, but I want to start off with making people see things they don't want to see, so they can get the help they need, make sense?"

Kevin saw his parents and Bart look uneasy before he took a deep breath. "Yeah, yah guess it does. Well, no easy way to do this, so might as well just dive in. Alison's right, better get going. So, unless I forgot something, time to get going. I'll contact you as soon as there is progress."

From there Kevin said his goodbyes to Bart and his parents, and even managed to share a warm embrace with his father. After making sure he had everything, he looked at Alison with as much confidence as he could muster. "So, ready for one hell of a road trip?"

Alison saw Kevin was trying not to look anxious, so she smiled and said "Oh, not keen on the long drive too much to be honest, but you know, just part of the job, right? Ready for a real pro tour?"

"Ready as I'll ever be. I'll try and not get too far behind."

"Don't worry, the roads may be long but straightforward. I know, this is a new thing for you so...I'll be a bit more forgiving than I would of some others."

"Thanks Alison, for everything."

"Oh, I guess I'm just a generous girl at times. Just don't forget it, okay Kevin?"

"Of course, Alison, I promise I'll never forget."

"You made it a little clear by now, Kevin. Devotion is something a lady hopes for in a guy, as long as it's the right kind. But you've proven you have the right kind of devotion in you, Kevin.

"Someone's obsessed when they just mindlessly want the same result, but someone's devoted when they see not what they want to see and react accordingly. You saw how things were and reacted, Kevin.

"Sometimes, maybe even a lot of times, things were outside your control. But you saw your chance and took it. Thankfully for you, I was looking for a change too, and we found out we could help each other make it before we missed our chance."

"Don't want to get all sappy but…does it almost feels like a dream coming true. Or maybe it's just that it's been so long since something has gone right that that itself feels like a dream."

"Oh, come on, Kevin, that is a *little* sappy. But it's okay, sometimes life has some sappy moments. Maybe life does not go how we plan it, but we've got to be ready for when things change, and we can shape things. It's like a dance or a tango, you can't control the dance, but just have to be ready to move to the beats when it's your time. Thankfully you don't seem like too bad a dance partner after all Kevin, with the right dance."

"Well, guess I can push myself to…"

To his shock, Alison put her hand over his lips before winking. "Kevin, you don't have to say what we both already know. It's really simple, I'm happy we were able to remember how well we work together."

"Oh Alison, thanks so much."

Kevin looked at Alison adoringly for a few moments as the two friends got closer to each other. For a few moments Alison looked like she was going to kiss him, till she suddenly pulled back and giggled. "Take it easy tiger, we don't have time to get side-tracked. Let's not get ahead of ourselves. But who knows…if this works out maybe we will hit the jackpot after all? C'mon partner, let's get this show on the road."

Alison gave Kevin a friendly tap on his shoulder, before heading to her car. Despite it not ending quite how he hoped, Kevin remained encouraged by Alison's friendly look as she got into her car. Kevin saw Bart and his parents give one last wave before he waved back and got into his own car.

He saw the ambulance drive past him before he took a deep breath, looked at his house one last time and grasped his wheel tightly as he got ready to start the next phase of his life.

Damn...after all these years of having dreams like this, this is really happening. I might be able to have a real career and a shot with Alison after all. Guess dreams can come true if you don't give up. Just got to do more than hope it will come true, and keep fighting every moment to hang on till that chance arrives. Not in the clear yet, but I'll do everything I can to make sure I can keep up with the American Tango, no matter how fast this dance gets.

Made in the USA
Middletown, DE
02 July 2021

43495333R00126